When Love Finds You Twice

When Love Finds You Twice

THOMAS BEZOMBE

Thomas Bezombe
contact@thomasbezombe.com
www.ThomasBezombe.com

When Love Finds You Twice

First Edition • December 2025

ISBN Print: 979-8-218-85470-6
ISBN Ebook: 979-8-9940979-0-8

Cover Image by Thomas Bezombe
Cover Design by Thomas Bezombe
Interior Design by Thomas Bezombe
Bird symbol created by Freepik from Flaticon.com

ACKNOWLEDGMENTS

Three amazing people helped with this book along the way, and they deserve my deepest and most sincere gratitude. I would like to thank Kevin Pirela, for his considerable critique of the countless drafts this story has seen and for constantly pushing it to greater heights. I would also like to thank Sofia Rodriguez for lending me her expertise and giving me some much needed feedback. And I would like to thank my wife, Alejandra Espinel, for being my peace and for her unwavering support of me. This story wouldn't exist without these three wonderful people.

And I realize there's no shortage of wickedness in the
world…but is it not heartening to know that so many
are willing to fight for the good?

—Trenton Lee Stewart, *The Mysterious Benedict Society
and the Perilous Journey*

PROLOGUE

On my first day of middle school, my mom shared some much-needed wisdom: she told me that the key to making friends was to take something that I loved and show it off to my classmates. The only thing I liked was collecting baseball cards, so I took out my favorite cards and laid them out in front of me on my desk. It was lunchtime and I still hadn't talked to anyone, but I held on to hope that my luck would change. The last thing my ten-year-old self would have expected was that the first person to talk to me was going to be such a pretty girl.

"Hey, are those baseball cards?" the girl asked sweetly. I couldn't help but stare up at her, alarmed. It might've been due to me being so little at the time, but I believed the girl to be the most beautiful girl I had ever seen. Her green eyes had a hypnotic effect on me, the kind that made you forget the entire English language at the drop of a hat.

"Yes, they are," I sputtered out at once. I couldn't tell if the girl realized how nervous I was, but she didn't show it. She flashed a warm smile, one that made my heart beat faster.

"These are all famous players, right? I imagine so, since they have cards made about them, right? Do you have a favorite?"

I felt as if I was being interrogated. No one had ever asked me three questions in a row without waiting for me to answer any of them before. And yet, I couldn't have enough of it. The girl could've asked me for my medical history and I'd have divulged it without a second thought.

"This one, he's my favorite. He could pitch a 100 mile per hour fastball," I said, feeling much calmer. Talking about my baseball cards helped me hide my quickening heartbeat.

"One hundred miles per hour? That's fast! I'd love to see that in person. Someone that can throw a ball that fast must be so cool!"

I blinked at the girl multiple times as I processed what she said.

"You think that a guy pitching 100 miles per hour is cool—" I started to ask, but she leaned into me just an inch to peer over my shoulder to look at the cards, which put an end to my entire train of thought.

"I don't really like to collect anything, so I admire people that do. I think it's nice," she sighed. I wanted to keep talking to her about it, to keep the conversation going at all costs.

But when she stood back up again, what she said next was the last thing I ever expected.

"You don't recognize me, huh? You live on the same street I live on. I saw you on the bus stop up my street."

I stared at her, my mind a blank canvas.

She giggled quietly. "Your head was always low, and your eyes never left the ground! It's no surprise that you didn't see me waiting next to you for the bus."

Just then, another girl pulled her away by the arm playfully. "Sorry, have to go! Nice to meet you, and nice cards!"

I watched as the girl left and kept staring at where she was long after she was gone. A small seed was planted in me at that moment, a seed that I would continue to nurture as the years went by, and I grew older.

Part of that seed was the motivation to become a pitcher, with the sole goal of throwing a 100 mile per hour fastball. But there was another side to that seed. And that other side consisted of the feelings I began to feel for that wonderful girl with green eyes.

1

The panic had begun to settle in. I was in my senior year at Fall River High, and I couldn't shake the feeling that I was running out of time. That question people asked you when you were young, "What do you want to be when you grow up?" My response to it had always been a blank stare. My name is Clara Monroe, and I had never been able to truly answer that question for myself.

My mom had always been big on my grades even though she was working multiple jobs out of necessity. Even when I was sure I could let a failed exam slip past her radar, she'd catch me when my guard was down and tell me she knew about it. Leave it to the parent portal to divulge all of my slipping grades to my mother. Most of all, though, she was worried that I wasn't showing any interest in anything. She'd ask me what I wanted to do for work, and I just couldn't come up with an answer.

When I hit sophomore year, things changed. I began to obsess over the local newspaper in my town. My mom couldn't afford a subscription to the paper for home delivery, so I waited excitedly until the weekly paper dropped so that I could go to my local general store and buy the paper. I'd love to read the columns, casually browse the different local businesses paying for advertisements, and of course laugh at the comic section. It became a weekly routine and before I knew it, I wanted to learn more about the paper and journalism in general. There was something about reading about your hometown that made you feel more connected to it, and the journalists behind the paper seemed to have captured that magic perfectly.

When I told my mother about my interest in journalism, I thought she'd tell me to focus on my grades instead. I just know that it would've crushed sophomore-age Me's hopes, and I'd have dropped the idea entirely. To my surprise, she was thrilled. She was singing in the shower for days, probably because she felt I wouldn't drift through life aimlessly anymore.

I was already awake when my morning alarm went off. I moved over to silence it, and my mom lingered by the door as she was walking by. "Honey, I understand two or three alarms. But five? It's like you're torturing yourself with that sound. I hear it from the kitchen."

"It's just in case I overslept," I shrugged up my shoulders innocently. "Mom, did you have time to get those groceries?"

"Oh, sweetheart, I completely forgot," she answered with a disappointed look on her face.

I got on my hands and knees and tried to fish out my bookbag from under my bed. "That's ok, mom, whenever you have time." I didn't say it, but I had already deciphered that when she said she didn't have time, it meant she hadn't been able to muster enough money for groceries just yet.

My mom noticed me struggling and got on her knees beside me. She did that annoying parent thing where she instantly found the thing I was looking for, pulling my bookbag out effortlessly and handing it to me.

"I can get another job afterschool you know. Something that will pay me more," I told her, sitting up. I caught guilt flash on her face. I knew how hard she worked to put food on the table and the lengths she went through to hide it from me. The exhaustion she felt was evident just by looking at her face.

"Honey, what I need you to do is focus on your grades and graduate. What you're doing for the newspaper is more than enough. Don't worry about me…I'm making things work just fine," she answered as she gave me a soft kiss on my forehead.

The financial problems my mom is forced to deal with is because of my dad, who racked up a ton of debt and then split. He ran off and dumped the debt onto my mom, forcing her to work all sorts of jobs to manage the debt and pay for food. I always made sure to thank her for what she does for me, even though she tried to be subtle about it.

At the start of my senior year, I started a part-time job as an assistant editor at my local paper. The schedule is flexible, and I did my best to manage my time with work and school. I couldn't help that my grades slipped slightly. It was nothing I couldn't handle, and I knew that didn't compare to what my mom did for me. The job didn't pay very much, and I knew that there were jobs that could pay me more. But, selfishly, I wanted to do anything that would allow me to be closer to the paper. It was just a desk job in the beginning, and all I did was proofread and edit articles for grammar, and sometimes write filler material and short summaries, but it was still a blast for me.

Even though I wasn't sure if it was what I wanted to do for the rest of my life, I had begun to fall in love with the idea of becoming a community reporter. Sometimes, when I watched the reporters at work on the field or in the office, I'd wonder to myself if I was smart enough to ask the right questions, and if I was brave enough to get into any sort of situation to get the story. It was a paralyzing feeling, the fear that I lacked the spark that reporters seemed to grasp so naturally. Part of me believed that if I became a reporter, it wouldn't just help me figure out if I loved it, but it would also force the world to tell me if I belonged in that world.

For now, all I got and planned to do was admire it from a distance.

"Hm?" my mother said as something caught her attention. "Hey, remember this?" she asked as she pulled out a shoebox from under my bed.

I looked at the box curiously, trying to remember what was inside of it. It was decorated with girly stickers like rainbows and pink stars.

"He's coming back to town this week, you know," she said with a mischievous look in her eyes.

I remembered the contents of the box with a start. Embarrassed, I shoved the box right under the bed. "*Mom*, I had forgotten all about it. Why did you have to remind me?"

Her eyebrows shoot up on her forehead. "Oh really, you just happened to forget that your childhood friend that moved away years ago is coming back to town this week? That's what you're telling me?"

I got up in a huff and hurriedly moved to finish getting ready for school. "That's what I'm telling you," I insisted.

"Hm, that's so strange, this calendar here on your desk has a large red circle around it for this week. Isn't that interesting?" she teased as she approached my desk.

"Mom!" I yelled at her as I threw a pillow at her back. "That's because the farmer's market is this Saturday, not because of anything else!"

She laughed playfully as she picked up the pillow from the ground.

"Besides, mom," I paused to take a quick look at myself in the body-size mirror in my room. "I haven't talked to him since he moved away. It's been four years. He probably hasn't thought of me at all."

My mom gave me a doubtful look. "I wonder," she said airily as she started to leave the room. She paused at the door and looked over her shoulder at me. "His mother says he's grown a lot since he moved away. I'm excited to see him."

After a quick breakfast, I said bye to my mom, who had finished getting ready for work. We headed out of the door at the same time, and she took great care in making sure to lock up. "Remember, I'm going to the farmer's market today after school," I reminded her.

"That's for the newspaper, right? Are you going to be reporting on it?"

"Some of my coworkers will be there, but I'm still just editing. The best editors can draw from their personal experience of being in the location, which is why they send me places along with the reporters."

"You going to get some quotes today?"

I made a face at the question. Although I had been eyeing being a reporter, something I struggled with was interviews. Since I wasn't an official community reporter yet, I always felt like I was playing pretend when I asked for quotes, even though the paper has told me they can use anything I get as well.

"Just do your best, sweetheart," she said before kissing my forehead again, her way of saying goodbye.

"And sweetheart," she said, suddenly serious. "Remember the curfew, you understand?"

I made a face. "Hasn't it been two weeks already? When are they going to lift that, mom?"

"I don't know, Clara. But I'm not messing around. Come straight home, be mindful of that curfew."

I watched her walk up the street before turning in the opposite direction and started walking towards the bus stop.

Luckily, the bus stop was right in front of my block, so I didn't have to walk far. As I walked towards it, my head instinctively drew itself to the left as I passed a certain house down the street. The house in question used to be the home of a boy named Silas Quinn, and like my mother kindly pointed out, he and I were childhood friends.

During all the block parties, birthdays, and even random afternoons where we were both bored with nothing else to do, Silas and I used to go to each other's houses. We'd meet up to play outside, make up games out of nothing, and in general just pass the time. Things were so simple back then, and part of me wished I could go back to those times.

If I had to pinpoint exactly when our friendship grew stronger, it would be when he covered for me during another neighbor's birthday party. She was our age, and for her present I promised I could cut her hair. I went to town with a pair of scissors, and I ruined her hair before any of the adults caught me. She went crying to her parents, and I knew I ruined everything. Well, there Silas was, claiming it had been him that cut that girl's hair.

"Why did you do it?" I asked. "Because you looked sad when she saw her reflection and cried. I knew you didn't do it on purpose," was his answer.

We continued to grow closer, and I started to feel like Silas was an irreplaceable, constant part of my life. I depended on him and counted on the fact that he'd always be around. It's for that reason that it came as such a shock to me when I heard about his parents' divorce. They were separating, and for reasons I didn't understand at the time, Silas was going with his father. Whether it was purposefully or not, he started to create some distance between us during the time leading up to his departure. I never got to properly say goodbye to him, something I had deeply regretted ever since. Silas and I were both 11 when we first met, and we enjoyed each other's company almost daily for three years. Four years had passed without a call or a letter, which made him 18 years old now.

Someone who I was so confident would be around forever disappeared suddenly, and I felt like an integral part of me had been ripped away. I was confident I'd think about him every day, but my thoughts for him burnt out slowly like a dying flame.

That was, until I heard that he was moving back.

I didn't have to wait at my bus stop for long. The bus arrived and I got on, choosing an available seat in the moderately crowded bus. The bus driver waited until I was seated before setting the bus in motion again.

As I looked out of the bus window at the passing scenery, I saw Fall River, the beautiful, small but mighty, and homey town that I've lived in my entire life. Fall River had a population of 15,000, and it showed. We only had two high schools to choose from, and almost everyone knew each other. There simply wasn't anything to do in a town this small. You just saw the same people, went to the same places, and it all ended up becoming monotonous. People in my school ended up having to travel to other nearby towns to be able to find anything fun to do.

I remember feeling envious of Silas when he got to move away to a big city while I got left behind. I wondered what sort of things he'd done and how much fun he'd been having so far away from here.

So far away from *me*, more like.

And yet, I thought to myself as I smiled, my eyes focusing on my slightly transparent reflection on the window. *I couldn't help but have fallen in love with it all.*

2

The low, powerful rumble of the Mustang's engine was a sound I had grown used to. I watched as the trees along the road flew past the passenger side window in a blur. Realizing I had been quiet for too long, I stopped looking at the window and looked over to my left at Caleb in the driver's seat, my hand loosely gripped by his over the center console.

Caleb Rhodes was a boy I'd been dating for the past 9 months. We started dating in our junior year, and it had been great thus far. I hadn't started dating him because he had his own car, but having a boyfriend with a set of wheels was great. I got to be chauffeured by him when he wasn't busy, which saved me from being limited to public transportation. He drove a white 1995 Mustang GT, which meant all of our friends groaned when they needed to depend on Caleb for a ride and I was already riding shotgun.

"Thanks for the ride again. I know you're missing a game," I told him.

He shifted his hand on the steering wheel, his eyes moving down from the road to the speedometer and back again. "Don't sweat it. But I just don't get why you needed to be there this early. I mean, it lasts from 9 in the morning until 1 in the afternoon, right?"

"The bus schedule is reduced on the weekends. The first bus starts at around 10, so I'd be getting there late," I reminded him. "And I have to be there right at 9 to recount the start of the event all the way to the end."

"They still have you just editing though, right?" Caleb asked. "When are they going to give you a chance to show your stuff?" I grinned at the question. Caleb had been about as desperate as I was when it came to waiting for me to get a chance to report on something. "Who knows. Today might be the day," I answered.

"At least editing is a step in the right direction, right?"

I laughed, looking over at him. "Sure, I think editing for the local paper is closer to being a reporter than working at an ice cream shop."

Caleb moved his hand from the top of the steering wheel, trying to peek at his speedometer again. "You have to admit, the free ice cream was sweet, though."

I rolled my eyes playfully, shifting in my seat comfortably. I adjusted the small bag resting on my lap. I carried all of my reporting equipment in it. It had a thin, spiral-bound notebook that I could hold comfortably in one hand. I was also equipped with many, many pens since they had a tendency to fail me when I needed them most. Most importantly of all, I always had a microcassette recorder in my bag. It was a small, handheld recorder that I could use during my interviews so that I could transcribe quotes exactly. The recorder was a loaner from the job, but I hoped to have my own one day.

Turning into the large unpaved field adjacent to the farmer's market, Caleb pulled into an empty space and killed the engine. Caleb got out of the car first and waited for me to leave the car before he locked it. I made sure to close the door softly and carefully as usual. As we made our way through the rows of parked cars, I paused, tilting my head at the sleek, aggressively faired shape of a bike. You didn't see many motorcycles in Fall River, and certainly none that looked this fast. It looked too expensive and too fast for our small town. I wondered, automatically, who drove it. I had to suppress a quick, shallow thought that biker guys, cliché as it was, were undeniably hot.

I hitched my bag higher up on my shoulder as we approached the market. It was bustling despite its small size and early opening time. Standing at the entrance, you could easily scan the entire layout, a long, rough rectangle of activity stretching down the slightly overgrown grass. A few dozen tents, all adorned with the names of local businesses, formed the outer shape of the rectangle. The sight of it immediately brought a smile to my face, as it brought back memories of visiting markets like these with my mom, especially the thick, sweet smell of maple.

Near the entrance, one tent was completely dedicated to stacked jugs of deep amber maple syrup, alongside small, ornate jars of honey. The stall was manned by an older woman and two younger children, clearly a family business. I made a mental note to come back to the stall to try to include the sweet woman and her family in the paper.

Further down, another tent showcased tall crates brimming with gourds and winter squash next to bushel baskets overflowing with dark red McIntosh and Honeycrisp apples. I involuntarily grinned at the sight of the apples. Every once in a while, a memory of Silas came to me in a flash as I looked at a random object. Looking at these apples, I recalled one time that Silas's mother had bought him a McIntosh apple during a block party. He accidentally dropped it into a deep puddle, and even though he didn't cry and tried not to seem bothered, I could somehow see through him and knew just how upset he was.

I was filled with memories of moments when I could seemingly read Silas'ss thoughts even though he tried to hide them. He was always an open book to me, even though he was usually reserved with others.

I'm brought back to my senses as Caleb approached the tent and ordered a Honeycrisp apple. "Thank you," he said as he handed the cash over to the vendor. He started to take a bite from the apple when he looked over at me and froze mid bite. "Did you want one?" he asked innocently as he retracted the apple from his mouth. "I'm good," I answered as I started to scan the area for familiar faces.

Thinking back to when Silas dropped that apple, I had also gotten one from my mom during that party. I remembered sharing half of mine with Silas, even though he insisted he was fine without it. The look of happiness when I offered him half the apple brought a silent smile to my face, even as I stood in this bustling market.

The sound of the market was pleasant: the low murmur of voices talking as purchases were completed, paper bags rustling, and the faint, rhythmic click of a calculator and the clink of coins being counted out into an open cash box. The open field also allowed a loud breeze to swoosh by, and I instinctively pulled the collar of my jacket higher.

"Clara!" I heard someone call out my name. I turned to see my longtime best friend, Lauren Poppy, coming over. She waved excitedly, and I spotted a borrowed yearbook camera hanging around her neck and grinned at her.

"No problems borrowing the camera for something non-yearbook related, huh?" I leaned into her. "I have my methods," she responded with a wink.

Lauren and I became friends just after Silas moved away, so she never got to meet him. I told her all sorts of things about him, but as time moved on, her frequent questions about him did too.

I recall when Lauren asked me about Silas back when Caleb and I first got back together.

"What if Silas came back?" she had asked me with a mischievous glint in her eye. I just stared back at her, confused. "What does Silas have to do with anything?" I answered.

Lauren walked up to me and started pulling my arm. "Shall we get started on your reporting? Sooner we get started, the quicker we'll finish, right?" I nodded at her, feeling more confident now that she was by my side. "I see a few of my coworkers, we should let them know that we're here. Caleb, do you mind—"

"Don't worry about me," he cut me off. "You do your thing. I'll be around, let me know when you need a ride. Lauren, are you going to be coming with—"

"No thanks," Lauren answered as she narrowed her eyes slightly. "Your backseat still gives me claustrophobic nightmares sometimes."

Lauren got into photography about the same time that I started getting interested in journalism, so we became a match made in heaven. As she improved in her photography, she became more and more of an asset to me. Even though she didn't have a camera of her own and needed to borrow one from the school's yearbook club, she'd become proficient and highly dependable. It was rare that I'd get the chance to report on anything and needed a photographer, but Lauren was always there when I needed her.

After stopping to check in with the community reporter responsible for the market, he gave Lauren and me an admiring glance. "You two are early, that's great. Go ahead and get some interviews and quotes as if you were doing the real deal. The editors might like your stuff and use it, so give it your all."

With that word of encouragement, Lauren and I got

to work. We started by photographing the farmers market and interviewing different subjects. I was the one that mostly framed the shots; however, occasionally she suggested a shot of her own. I smiled internally, knowing that when I looked back at the shots she took, I'd inevitably end up liking the ones she suggested above my own.

Like I originally planned, I returned to the family-owned maple syrup business after a few hours. I kindly asked to feature them in the local newspaper, and they readily agreed. I interviewed the woman and the children, making sure my microcassette recorder was running. They offered a sample of their syrup, which I hungrily agreed to try. I jokingly told them that their bribery attempt wouldn't work on me, even though it most certainly did.

In the corner of my eye, I spotted their cash box. The lockable metal box was particularly filled with cash, and it made me immensely happy to know that the farmers market proved to be a good turnout for their business. Lauren and I thanked them for their time before taking our leave.

"You see, you did great Clara," Lauren chirped happily.

I sighed. "I don't know, it still feels like I'm an imposter when I ask questions."

Lauren shook her head from side to side. "I don't know what it'll take to open your eyes."

"I think we have enough," I told Lauren over my shoulder, trying to change the subject. I felt accomplished by the quotes we had, confident that

Lauren's photos were up to par. I gave her a look of triumph which she returned, letting me know she felt the same way.

"Geez, he's getting another one?" Lauren groaned beside me. I looked forward and smiled pleasantly as I saw Caleb in the Honeycrisp tent again, another apple in his hands. There were a few people around him. I was about to approach Caleb and open my mouth to poke fun at him—

But his head suddenly jerked in my direction, his eyes focused intensely on something behind me. I heard a rush of commotion behind me, and voices were starting to increase in intensity. The familiar voice of the kind older woman called out, and I turned around with the feeling of my stomach dropping.

Two men were at the syrup stand, pulling and clawing at the cash box as the woman tried her best to prevent them from taking it. The two younger children watched in horror as the woman continued to call out, desperate. It wasn't long before they managed to pull the box free at last. They turned to the parking lot and started running, sprinting at full speed. Since the syrup booth was right at the entrance, it wasn't far for them. Other people started to give chase, but it was clear no one around that area could catch up to them.

A sense of helplessness flooded my body as I watched the cash box being taken away. Suddenly, I saw a blur of movement beside me—

In the next instant, I saw a guy standing next to me, in a position I recognized as mid-baseball pitching position. His eyes contained an intensity to them that burned more fiercely than anything I'd ever seen before; they looked focused enough to kill. The guy held a baseball within his fingertips, and before I could process what he was about to do, his body became a frenzy of raw power as he released the baseball at a breakneck speed. My eyes were rendered hopeless in tracking the ball as it blitzed through the air directly towards the thief that held the cash box. The ball flew directly to his head…

And it connected, causing the man to stop in his tracks and fall straight to the ground, along with the cash box. The box fell hard, opening and letting all of the bills contained inside fly out.

The second man looked at the cash desperately, frantically reaching out to grab a few bills before abandoning the first thief and taking off running again. The first thief squirmed in the ground before making another attempt to get to his feet, but it was too late for him. He was pinned back to the ground by other bystanders, and the cash box was once again secured.

"That's some arm," I heard Caleb mutter from behind me. "Clara, I'm going after them," he told me before taking off running. He made sure to stop at the syrup stand. "I'm going to follow them, please call the police," he huffed as he ran towards the parking lot. I saw a large pickup truck peel out from the farmers' market, followed by the sound of Caleb's Mustang roaring to life. I couldn't see the Mustang, but I heard it as Caleb took off from the market and started to chase the truck.

Feeling rooted to the spot, I mechanically looked

over to Lauren beside me. Her camera was lifted, and she was looking through the viewfinder. She lowered it from her face and looked at me with her mouth in an "o" shape.

"Don't tell me you got that," I sputtered. "Clara, I did," she managed.

Feeling the excitement starting to come down, I finally set my eyes on the guy who threw the baseball. His body was now relaxed, and there was a look of slight disappointment in his eyes, as if he wasn't satisfied by the outcome. As I looked at him, I felt my heart start to beat slightly faster. I felt drawn to him, intrigued immensely about who this guy was. The thing that caught my attention the most was that I felt that I recognized that pitching form, as if it had been ingrained in my memory. After sighing deeply, he turned to the entrance and started walking away, his hands in his pockets.

"Clara, hey, did you just get that?" the community reporter asked me, though he mostly directed the question to Lauren. She nodded hysterically, her eyes wide. "I also interviewed the family in that tent before this happened," I followed up. The reporter raised an eyebrow at me.

"I also have the interview on cassette player too," I added. "Ok, you win," he said as he lifted his hands up in defeat. "Listen, I need you to write a story on this for the newspaper. You have the photographer and the connection with the victims already. Listen, this is your first big break, so don't blow it."

I was frozen, unable to process what he just told

me. It was only after he left that Lauren started to grab my arm and shake me giddily. "We got the story! We're going to write on the paper, Clara!"

Suddenly coming to my senses, I jolted my head toward Lauren. "Lauren, I need to interview the guy, the one that threw the baseball." Lauren lifted an eyebrow and lowered her chin slightly. "You're going to interview that hottie? You don't need a photo of him by any chance, right?"

I rolled my eyes and started jogging to the entrance. "Good luck!" she called out to me. "It's not like that!" I answered over my shoulder. "I have a boyfriend!"

I made it to the unpaved field and started trying to find where the guy was. Luckily, I didn't have to look for him for long. Eventually, I caught him beside the motorcycle that caught my attention earlier. Go figure. I took a moment to quickly try to fix my hair, though I didn't realize I was doing it at the time.

I approached the guy from the side. He'd already put his bike helmet on and had his visor down, so I couldn't get a good look at his eyes just yet. I looked down towards his bike and noticed the words Kawasaki ZX-6R written boldly on the side. He saw me approaching and sat up a bit straighter on the bike.

Soundlessly, he lifted his visor and started to stare at me as I walked up to him. I couldn't put my finger on it, but it looked as if there was astonishment in his eyes. Even with the visor lifted, it was hard to tell for sure.

"Hi there!" I stammered, feeling somewhat nervous for a reason I couldn't explain. "I'm a reporter for the local newspaper and wanted to know if you could comment on what just happened here. I'd really appreciate a quote."

"Reporter?" he asked. Hidden behind his helmet, his eyes seemed to try to devour me whole. I felt my heartbeat quicken slightly as he continued to investigate every inch of my body with his gaze. With a relaxed series of movements, the guy kicked his leg over his bike to dismount it. He stood with his back turned to me as he cooly removed his helmet and adjusted his hair before turning around.

"That won't be a problem," he said huskily. "Considering we live on the same street again."

My heart started to do summersaults in my chest, all of the air leaving my lungs as I realized the guy standing in front of me is Silas Quinn. As casually as ever, Silas walked up to me and bent over at the waist so that we'd be eye-level. I tried my best to keep my eyes on his, but I couldn't manage it; they focused on anything except for those unwavering eyes of his.

Silas didn't move for many moments. "Hm," he murmured eventually. His eyes never left my own.

He's so close.

"I understand," Silas said standing up straight again. He walked back towards his bike and kicked his leg over it again. "Nothing's changed."

I wanted to ask him what he meant about that, but Silas turned the key to the ignition and the roar of the engine drowned out my voice effortlessly.

"Come over to my house tomorrow morning," he said as he put his helmet back over his head.

Where did he get this confidence from? I thought. *What if I had plans tomorrow? What would he have done then?*

"I—I can do that," I managed to respond. I was worried he wouldn't hear me over the sounds of the engine, yet he seemed to hear me. That, or he just knew how I'd respond. "Good," he answered.

"Looking forward to it, *Ms. Reporter*," he teased. I watched wordlessly as he backed out from the spot and took off, leaving me alone in the grassy field.

I started to breathe for what felt like the first time in a long time. I unconsciously brought a hand to my chest, trying to slow the panicked, unfamiliar race of my heart. I had forgotten it even knew how to beat that fast.

3

"I'm off, mom," I called out before I headed out of the door. "Oh! Are you going over to say hi to Silas?" she asked giddily from the kitchen. "It's for an interview for work, mom. I already told you."

The groan my mom made wasn't hard to miss; she wasn't trying to be subtle. "Bye mom!" I called out one last time. "Say hi to his mother for me!" she yelled before I closed the door.

I tried to calm my nerves as I walked down my street. It was the same street as always, and yet I felt a renewed sense of anxiety I didn't usually feel. Realizing how hard I was gripping my bag, I loosened my grip and tried to take deep, calming breaths.

Seeing Silas again after so long was surprising, sure. But it was his *transformation* that caught me off guard most of all. The maturity of his face, the impressive build that was visible even through his loose-fitting jacket. Most breathtaking of all was the seriousness of his eyes…

Tried as I might, I couldn't see any resemblance of the young Silas that I knew from my childhood. Through that rough and mature exterior, I couldn't help but wonder just what Silas has been through to sunset that younger version of him that I once knew.

Most of all, the fact that he told me that *Nothing's changed* drove me crazier than I would ever admit. It kept me up for the majority of the previous night, and tried as I might, I couldn't figure out what he meant.

Did he mean me? Was he saying I hadn't changed all of these four years?

The thought made my blood boil. The audacity! I happened to think that I had changed quite a bit in those four years, thank you very much. Not just in appearance but in maturity, too. There I was, noticing all sorts of changes in him, and yet there he was, claiming I hadn't changed at all!

Before I knew it, I was in front of his front door. I swallowed hard, working through what I was going to say to him. I steeled myself and knocked on the door, my raps on the door growing quieter and quieter, just like my resolve.

Silas's mother opened the door, which I was relieved about. "Hi sweetie! Oh, I'm so happy to see you!" she said as she pulled me into a hug. "Hi Ms. Monzon, long time no see," I managed to say with my face buried in her chest.

"Oh, please, call me Lisette. Come on in, you here to see Silas?" she asked innocently. "Yes, didn't he tell you? It's for the newspaper." Her eyes widened in surprise.

"That's right! You work for the local paper! Oh, I'm so proud of you. When I heard from your mother, I just couldn't wait to tell Silas over the phone about it."

Huh, I thought to myself. *That meant that he already knew about it before we ran into each other.*

"Sweetie he's not home right now. He told me he had a quick errand to run. God knows if he had told me you were coming, I'd have tied him to a chair until you got here."

She gestured to take a seat on the couch beside her, which I accepted. "I thought he'd let you know." Lisette exhaled from her nose quietly. "Oh, that boy doesn't tell me anything. He's been distant ever since he moved away, that one. Tells me the bare minimum to know that he's safe so I don't call the cops and file a missing person's report on him."

I let my eyes wander the room. I spotted a set of framed pictures on a low coffee table by the couch, which I leaned in to see. All of them were exclusively about Silas. I saw Silas as I remembered him, a young boy full of wonder. The pictures jumped to when he was much older, already looking slightly more jaded. The latest photos were of Silas with the same bike he had now, and his eyes contained the same seriousness I saw yesterday.

"Why did he move away, Lisette? I always knew about your divorce. But if you don't mind me asking, can I ask why he had to go?"

I watched as her eyes grew shades darker as

tiredness began to seep in. "Well Clara, you know this already, but Silas's father took a job and moved. He was always the breadwinner in our family, and I knew that I'd be struggling financially once he left. I thought I was doing the best thing for Silas by letting him go with him…"

Lisette chuckled to herself, but it lacked any sort of humor. "Which is something that I know Silas resents me for." Lisette took a minute, deep in thought. She looked at me after a beat and continued. "You're probably wondering why he's back now suddenly, right?"

Unable to find any words, I simply nodded at her as my reply. "Well, sweetie, I'm asking myself the same thing. Silas's relationship with his father wasn't always the best, but for a reason I don't know, Silas's fights with his father have been escalating lately. The next thing I knew, I was getting a phone call from Silas telling me he's coming home."

Just then, my head jerked to the side as I heard the front door slam open. Silas stumbled in through the door. "Ah, just the two women I was looking for," he said as he headed straight to the kitchen.

"Oh my god," Lisette mumbled as she got to her feet and rushed deeper into the house. She came back with a first aid kit in hand, which caused me to get to my feet in a rush. I followed behind Lisette and approached Silas, only to barely stop the audible gasp that almost escaped my mouth.

Upon closer inspection, I could see that Silas was bleeding from his mouth. He spat into the sink, leaving behind a hauntingly big blood splatter. I inspected his knuckles and saw his left knuckles were bloody and red. I investigated his right knuckles and, as my intuition told me, they were better and looked normal. Whatever the reason was that Silas got into a fight, he subconsciously made sure to avoid using his pitching hand and damaging it in any way.

"Another fight? Are you serious?" Lisette asked in a whisper.

"'Tis but a flesh wound, mother," he joked, smiling to reveal his blood-stained teeth. "Be quiet before I lock you in a room so that you stop getting into trouble," Lisette huffed as she opened her first aid kit and started treating his knuckles and his cheek.

"Trust me, I'm no stranger to that," he said under his breath as his gaze met my own. He suddenly grew serious, those eyes of him seemingly acknowledging me for the first time. "You're here?" he asked.

"You said 'Just the two women I was looking for' when you walked in. You sure that fight didn't knock the sense out of you?" I asked, my brow furrowed. I felt angry at how he had talked back to his mother and worried her. I had never seen Lisette, the sweet lady that she is, so panicked and afraid. To think that he had done this to her more than once didn't sit right with me. He continued to stare at me vacantly until I gave in. "You agreed to meet me for an interview," I sighed.

"Ah, yes, that's right. Mother, I'm going to be inviting the lady to my room, if there aren't any complaints," he whispered playfully. "As long as you behave," she answered sternly.

"Thanks for this," he said airily as he lifted his bandaged hand. He then started walking around the kitchen island. My eyes might have betrayed me, but it seemed like he lingered next to me for just a brief second before he kept moving. My breath hitched for just that brief moment that our bodies were just ever so closer together.

"You coming, *Ms. Reporter?*" he teased as he walked right out of the kitchen without looking back. "Don't you worry, sweetie," Lisette told me as she cleaned up the blood from the sink. "He's harmless, believe me."

I don't know about that, I answered in my head. "Pardon me," I told her as I started making my way out of the kitchen. "Oh, also, my mom says hi."

Lisette paused, her eyes glazing over as she suddenly straightened up. "I haven't spoken to your mother in a while. I should really give her a call. Go on ahead, sweetie. It's the last room on the right."

I made my way through the hall beside the kitchen and hunted down the last doorway. Silas had kindly left the door open, so I just walked in.

Silas stood in the center of the room beside his bed and was in the middle of removing his shirt. I froze at the doorway; my eyes widened in surprise as I looked at his exposed back. I caught myself in the next instant, and I started to reprimand him for changing knowing that I was following in behind him.

Just as his head passed through his shirt, I could see Silas bearing a pained expression, one that I knew he was trying hard to suppress. When he looked over at me in the doorway, he instantly changed his face into one of muted indifference. I realized then that he'd been hiding just how much pain he was in from the moment he walked in through the door.

I tried my best to move past the sight of Silas's bare back and took the first few steps into the room. I looked around quickly, surprised to be met with the same room of Silas's that I've remembered from when he was a kid. It seemed that in the few days he'd been back, he hadn't made any changes to it. I walked up to his desk and noticed a neatly stacked pile of baseball cards in the corner. Just beside the cards was a baseball cap with a familiar logo on it.

"Surprised it hasn't changed at all?" Silas mused. "Yeah, I am," I replied. I moved over to his bed and lingered, waiting for him to give me permission to sit. He tilted his chin up, a sign that said *Go ahead*. I sat and let my eyes wander the room again, looking for any excuse to avoid looking Silas directly in the eyes. I still wasn't over the fact that he invited me to his room; I had thought we would just talk in the kitchen.

"I don't care for it," Silas said as he pulled out his desk chair and positioned it just beside the bed to sit on. "It's not like I'm going to be here all that often—"

"I've always liked your room," I interjected. I forced my eyes to focus on Silas's. He looked at me with an expression that I can't figure out, and he leaned back on his chair while placing his arm over it lazily. "You had questions for me, right? Shoot."

"Before that," I said, my eyes looking at the baseball cap on Silas's desk again. "That bird logo…Isn't that your cap from the team you played with back in middle school?"

Silas didn't move; he immediately knew which cap I was talking about. "You remember, huh?" I rolled my eyes. "Of course I do. It's not something you just forget."

I adjusted myself on the bed. "You—You still play?"

"I don't have much of a choice," he answered as he craned his neck to the side. He looked detached; making it clear that he didn't want to spend any more time on the topic.

"Sure," I said awkwardly.

I pulled out my small spiral notebook from my bag and one of my pens. Without asking for his permission, I set my recorder on the bed beside myself and hit record. Silas raised an amused eyebrow at the recorder but didn't say anything. "I'm writing a story on the incident that happened yesterday at the farmer's market; the attempted theft of the cash box. You played a vital role in getting that cash box back. Can you tell me—"

"I didn't do anything heroic," Silas cut me off. "I just saw the first opportunity to pitch a baseball at someone's head without getting in trouble, and I went for it. Nothing more to it."

Silas looked up at his ceiling, deep in thought. "Though looking back, I still subconsciously held back on that throw. I should've given it everything I had just to see what would've happened."

"Silas, even if your intentions weren't directly to help, your actions still ended up helping others. That family that got their cash box returned even asked me to try to set up a meeting with you so they could thank you personally—"

"No, no, trust me I am not going to be thanked for beaming a baseball at some guy's head," Silas scoffed. "Besides, I didn't get all of the cash back. It was the guy in the Mustang that went after them, right? He's the hero, have them thank him personally."

I froze, my pen mid stroke. My body felt like it was suddenly rigid. I hadn't been expecting Silas to mention Caleb at all, and I was left wondering if I should talk about him or avoid bringing him up.

Do I tell Silas that Caleb is my boyfriend? I asked myself. *That's ridiculous, of course I'm going to tell him.*

"Yes, that was Caleb, he chased after the second thief after he ran away. He told me that he lost the truck after the driver took some strange off-road paths. It was reported to the police." I coughed, unsure how to phrase what I had to say next. "Caleb is also…erm…my boyfriend."

Silas's face was a mask. I looked at it intently to try to gauge any sort of change in his expression, and yet I didn't see any changes at all. The only thing I caught was a small twitch on the side of Silas's mouth as it turned downward, but it only lasted for the blink of an eye.

After a beat of silence, Silas egged me on, using his head as a signal urging me to go on. "Right. Silas, do you always have a baseball on you? It was lucky that you had one at the time of the incident, and I'd like to know if this was a coincidence or if it was habit."

I noticed Silas's expression darken significantly at the question. "A habit passed on from my father, let's leave it at that."

"Is there any reason—"

"You know what?" Silas talked over me. "If you're going to report on the attempted theft at the market, you should highlight the increase in crime that's been happening in this town. I've run into nothing but trouble as soon as I got here. I mean, I got into a fight at a gas station before even getting into Fall River."

I opened my mouth, intrigued, but Silas cut me off. "And since when is there a curfew here? Everyone under the age of 21 has to be indoors before 8 PM? When was that implemented? What's the deal with that?"

I blinked at him in confusion. "The police said it was to reduce disorderly conduct among teenagers and young adults after dark. There's been an uptick in graffiti reports and noise complaints in public areas. The curfew's been in place for about two weeks now."

"You're crazy if you think I'm obeying that," Silas scoffed.

I lifted a hand up in surrender. "Wait, back up. you said you got into a fight at a gas station? Where was this?"

Silas looked caught off guard by my interest. He settled himself into a different sitting position. "Yeah, that was the other fight my mother was talking about. During the last stretch before getting here, between Fall River and Arden Bay, I got involved in something."

"Between Arden Bay and Fall River…" I trailed off.

"Hey, listen," Silas paused, massaging his neck. "I was just venting, it's probably nothing—"

"No, you're saying you've noticed something, and I want to investigate," I cut him off. I returned his confused expression with a serious one.

"I could be wrong; it's probably nothing serious."

"I trust your intuition. Can we leave it at that?" I asked, feeling somewhat embarrassed. Silas took a moment to give any sort of reaction. After a beat, he started stretching backwards as if nothing had just happened.

"Listen, if you looked at a map, could you tell me exactly where that gas station was? As soon as possible, too, please." Silas jerked forward, hands on his knees. "You want me to look at a map and try to find that same exact gas station…just for your story?"

"I'll be at the office for the rest of the day. You know the address of the local paper, right? I'll be waiting for you," I said without another word as I headed for the door. I only made it a few paces towards the door when Silas suddenly grabbed my hand. I turned to look over at him, surprised.

Silas laughed amusedly as he dropped my hand. He wordlessly got to his feet and rummaged around his drawer for a sheet of paper and a pen.

"The address, if you please," he said soothingly. I composed myself and grabbed the paper from him. I wrote down the address and left it on his desk. Just before I turned towards the door again, I grabbed the cap from the top of Silas's desk.

I turned toward him and placed the hat on his head, which Silas accepted without a fight.

"How does it still fit on your head?" I asked, taking a step back to admire how good it looked on him. "Just before I moved away, I bought a parents size so I could grow into it," Silas answered earnestly.

"It looks good on you," I said shyly. Feeling embarrassed, I turned back towards the door. I lingered at the doorway and faced him one last time. "Silas, I'm counting on you. Thank you."

Silas didn't give me much of a reply. He gave me an enticing look, one that he didn't break away from until I went out into the hall and a wall cut off our line of sight.

4

I could remember, clear as day, the first time that I watched Silas playing baseball. He and I were at a park by our house as kids, walking close enough that we could have been holding hands if either of us put our minds to it. Suddenly, someone called out Silas's name.

"Silas! We need one more person for baseball! Please, can you join us for a quick game?"

He wasn't too ecstatic about the idea, but even I could see the desperation in the boy's face. He looked close to crying as he pleaded with Silas to join the game. Silas looked over at me sheepishly, as if getting my approval before confirming he could join. I thought it was so cute that I couldn't tell him no, even though it wasn't like we were in the middle of a date or anything. It was just a hangout at the park, nothing more.

As I moved over to the edge of the field, I couldn't

help but wonder why that boy was so desperate for Silas to join them during their game. Was it truly just because they were missing a player, or because he saw Silas and wanted him desperately on his team?

I sat on the edge of the field expectantly, my eyes glued to Silas. They put a glove and a baseball in his hand and immediately put him on the pitcher's mound. As Silas took to the mound, I witnesses him change. He was usually an awkward boy, unsuited for a position where all eyes would be on him. But standing there, he suddenly looked exactly like he belonged. His face hardened, and that unserious face I had gotten used to seeing him have vanished into thin air.

The game began, and my eyes became wide as saucers as his very first pitch was executed with impressive precision. Even though his inexperience was obvious, there was determination and a fire in his eyes that made me feel something deep in my chest. For a reason I couldn't explain, I was so happy that I got to see that side of his that I thought about it for days and days.

I witnessed Silas's passion for baseball continue to grow as time went on. He continued to play games at the park with his friends and eventually joined a team. Even though he hadn't taken practice too seriously by that moment, his skill was clearly above those of the boys around him. It was inevitable that his father would eventually become aware of Silas's latent abilities.

"That boy is a prodigy," I heard Silas's father comment during a block party. The adults were all gathered, and I happened to hear it as I was trying to sneak a McIntosh apple for Silas. "I'm going to make sure he goes professional, where he deserves to be."

I consulted the dictionary in my house that night to look at what that word meant. As my eyes read the words, *highly talented child or youth*, quick flashes of Silas appeared in my brain immediately. I smiled wide enough that my cheekbones started to hurt, knowing that the boy I was close to was so dearly special.

***

Hunched over my computer in my office at the local paper, I transcribed the quotes I got from Silas and started working on the feature that I was assigned. The editor in charge of the story provided me with the space on the paper that would be dedicated to my story, and I'd managed to get a mockup of what I wanted the feature to look like. All I needed was the final piece of where that gas station was.

I sighed, exhausted, as I leaned back on my office chair. On Sundays, the paper was locked up and closed to the public. Even closed, though, the office space wasn't entirely empty. There was still a skeleton crew of editors and reporters still working, and I knew they were counting me to complete this feature for the issue that dropped on Monday.

I closed my eyes and prayed that Silas pulled through and came with that missing piece of information. I forgot to tell him that I needed it by today, so he might not come at all. Suddenly, I heard two sets of footsteps walk into the office.

"Clara? Someone was outside saying they have something for you," an editor called out. I clammed up, realizing that meant Silas had been let into the office. The few heads still in the office all suddenly turned to me, and I turned my head nervously to see Silas approaching me with a smirk on his face.

The person in the office desk next to me whispered in my ear: "Clara, is that your boyfriend? You finally brought him into the office, huh? He's cute." I coughed, shyly, unsure how best to address the mix-up.

Silas pulled out the chair beside mine and sat on it without hesitating. "I imagined you needed this today even though you didn't say so," he said matter-of-factly. "It wasn't easy, but here's your gas station." He pulled out a ripped sheet of paper with an address on it and the name of a gas station.

I read over the address with a blank expression, as if reading it would populate an image of the gas station in my mind. "This means a lot, Silas. Thank you, seriously," I told him sincerely. He looked satisfied and started to move like he's about to get back on his feet. I suddenly didn't want him to leave, so I asked him a question that had been on my mind. "Can you tell me what the fight you had there was even about? That'd help, too," I asked.

Silas looked bothered that I asked. He gave me a pensive look, as if he's weighing the consequences of sharing the answer with me. It took a beat, but in the end, he gave in.

"A young couple was being harassed at their gas pump. Three guys were hounding them to pay for their gas, asking for a donation." Silas pulled his shoulders back, cracking his back slightly. "They had a crying baby in the car, who was scared. That's why I got involved."

I looked at him, confused.

Why didn't he want to share that with me?

Feeling as if he'd accomplished what he came to do, Silas got right up and walked out of the office without another word.

"A man of few words, isn't he?" the person besides me asked. I smiled as I looked at her, sighing in agreement. Her name is Audrey Price, an experienced community reporter. Ever since I started working for the local paper, she'd been a great resource and turned any chance into a learning opportunity. She was much older than me, that much was clear. But I never bothered to ask her exactly what her age was.

Audrey looked over at the address and a few of the papers on my desk. She gave me a knowing look and returned to the work she had on her own desk. "I can tell you've got quite the story on your hands," she said. "Give it your best."

I returned my gaze to the mess of papers on my desk, knowing that was her way of motivating me to keep working hard. "Thanks, Audrey."

***

"Why do you get the regular milk over the chocolate

milk? It tastes so much worse," a classmate, Ralph, asked.

"It has less calories," Caleb replied. "Yeah, by what—ten? Are you serious, man?"

Ralph was Caleb's closest friend. The two of them played for Fall River's baseball team. He played mostly for fun, while Caleb always saw baseball as a career.

"I have to side with Ralph on this one. The regular milk doesn't taste like anything," Lauren added. "Thank you," Ralph said with a satisfied look on his face.

I smiled at the tray in front of me. Ralph looked beyond happy that Lauren agreed with him, even over something as dumb as milk flavors. Ralph had asked Lauren out on a date more times than I could count, but she had always turned him down. It wasn't hard to see that he had still been holding out hope of her mind changing, though.

Caleb, Lauren, and Ralph were the usual suspects that I ate with during lunchtime. We had a designated table in the courtyard area just outside the cafeteria. There was one person missing from our group: Emmy. She had told us she'd be a bit late, so we started eating without her.

"Caleb, you talk to that guy you told me about from the farmer's market?" Ralph asked. The sudden change of topic made me almost choke on my food. I tried to hide my coughing fit, but Caleb gave me a look. Lauren patted my back, more a sign of consolation rather than an attempt to help my inability to breathe.

"No, but I plan to this week. I don't know where

he's transferred from, but I hear today's his first day." I nearly choked on my food again. "He starts today? He's here?" Lauren asked excitedly.

"Our team's is missing a star pitcher, we've got to get him to join, man," Ralph urged.

Lauren looked over at me with her eyes beaming, dying to tell me something but I knew she couldn't because Caleb was sitting right beside me. The feeling of hiding something from him didn't sit right with me. I made up my mind to tell him of my previous history with Silas before things got messy. I opened my mouth to start to explain when Ralph suddenly got to his feet. "What's going on over there?" he asked.

I turned to see a crowd forming on the edge of the courtyard. I started to feel a deep sense of alarm cementing itself in my entire body. I got to my feet and started heading towards the circle, Lauren right on my heels.

I pushed my way to the center of the circle to see Emmy on the ground, her books and bookbag on the floor. Her eyes were wide in astonishment, staring fixedly above herself. I looked up to see Silas standing right above her, his hand clenching another boy's shirt collar tightly. The boy standing in front of Silas was looking back at him furious, while Silas returned the look with one of pure boredom.

"Hey!" Lauren shouted at the near top of her lungs. "Which one of you is messing with my friend?!" she stomped up to the two boys and pointed down at Emmy.

Silas didn't break eye contact with the other boy, but

jerked his head to the side, pointing it at Emmy on the ground. "You going to help her pick those up?" he asked menacingly.

"Get off," the other boy responded, his voice low and cold. "You stuck out your foot to trip the girl. I saw the entire thing," Silas answered.

The boy gave Silas an agitated look. "I'm telling you it was an accident!" he shouted as he pushed Silas roughly. Silas let go of his grip and took a step backward.

"Hey, break it up," Caleb called out as he entered the circle.

"*You?*" Silas and Caleb said at the same time as their eyes met. In the next instant, Silas scanned the crowd. I didn't know how, but I knew the person he was looking for was me. His eyes found mine, and an expression I couldn't decipher flashed on his face. He didn't waste any time before pushing through the crowd and leaving the circle at the point furthest away from where I stood.

I looked back down to ground as Lauren was helping Emmy back to her feet. The other boy that was confronted by Silas picked up the books that were scattered on the ground and handed them to Emmy.

"What do you think you're doing?" Lauren stood right up to the boy, who suddenly started to stammer. "I—I, uh—"

"You ever do something to her again, you won't get off so easily," she warned, her eyes cold and unwavering. The boy looked back at her, speechless. It was hard to say if he was intimidated by her, considering Lauren wasn't all that tall nor that threatening.

"Hey, go talk to him before he leaves. I'll handle his," I caught Ralph tell Caleb. Curious to hear how their conversation went, I followed loosely behind Caleb. Silas headed up a flight of stairs, which made a turn halfway up. Caleb caught up to Silas in the top half, giving me the chance to hide out on the bottom half out of their line of sight. I was able to hear their conversation easily from there.

I missed the beginning, but it was Caleb's voice that I heard first. "Listen, I saw how you threw that ball at the farmer's market. Why don't you join our team? We've got a good one but we're missing a pitcher like you."

I heard Silas respond with a harsh, humorless laugh. "That's going to be a no from me." It seemed like Silas was ready to leave the conversation there, because I heard footsteps as he continued up the stairs.

"Hey, wait—why not play for a team? You have skill, you should use it."

"You don't get to tell me what I should or shouldn't do," Silas responded bitterly. "I didn't come here to join some random high school team."

"Oh, so we're not good enough for you?" Caleb sounded insulted. "Are you too good to join our team, is that it?"

"What, you never get rejected before? Things usually go your way, is that it?" Silas gave a sarcastic laugh. "The only person I only play for is myself; I couldn't care less about your team."

Silas's response left me stunned, to the point where I didn't realize their conversation had been over. Caleb had started to come back down the stairs and before I knew it, he had spotted me. I froze, like a deer caught in headlights

"We should go rejoin the others," he muttered, his head hung low. I had a bizarre revelation: he seemed far more upset by Silas's harsh rejection than by my own awkward eavesdropping.

Just as I was starting to walk back to our cafeteria table, Lauren suddenly grabbed me by the arm and pulls me into the area beneath the stairwell, the go-to spot for additional privacy.

"So?" she asked about ready to explode in anticipation. "That guy," she paused, adding emphasis on the last word. "That's Silas, isn't it? That's the boy that lived on your street years ago, right?"

I took a deep breath, knowing there was no use in denying it. I nodded quietly as Lauren broke down into numerous undecipherable and excited squeals. "Oh, I knew this was going to happen! I asked you what if he came back while you were dating Caleb—"

"Wait, wait, this again? What does it matter that he's here?" Lauren gave me an exasperated look. "Um, hello? Do you need glasses or something? Are you not seeing how he looks? Did you not see how he stepped in and stood up for Emmy over someone tripping her?"

"Lauren, Silas was always just a friend. I don't even know if he has a girlfriend back wherever he's from. And I have a boyfriend, so...that's that. We might become friends again but that's what we always were."

Lauren shook her head in disappointment. Suddenly, she perked up with a question. "Did you ever tell Caleb about Silas?"

I squirmed uncomfortably. "I may have told him a bit about him. He was never too interested in hearing about it. I always got the impression he was jealous…"

"Of course he'd be jealous! You two were literally always together, Clara. You guys spent more time together than—"

"I'm telling you; it was always platonic," I said. "I never…erm…told him Silas's name, though. So, he doesn't know that Silas is…you know."

Lauren's eyebrow shot up in curiosity. "He doesn't know Silas is the boy from your past?"

I nodded at her. She started nodding slowly, letting the information sink in. I didn't have to say it, but I knew Lauren would keep the secret for me.

"… You guys would look *so* cute together."

"Not happening," I sighed with an eyeroll.

Lauren and I then started heading back to the table.

"By the way," I said. "You're still free after school to look at the issue, right?" Lauren looked over at me with a glint in her eye.

"I wouldn't miss that for the world."

"I could have shown you what the feature was going to look like before it got published, you know."

Lauren smiled as she looked out into the distance in front of her. "Nah, I prefer it this way. I'm going to see it for the first time right on the paper."

I nudged her in the shoulder playfully. "Hope you

like how I put everything together."

"I already know I will," she answered as she linked her arm through mine.

5

"He came over to your job, and you went over to his house?" Caleb asked me, surprised.

Caleb, Ralph, Emmy, Lauren and I were all walking to the nearest general store after school to buy and read the latest issue of the paper. Since Caleb was going to be reading about my interview with Silas, I didn't want to keep anything from Caleb any longer. Though I intended to tell him he was the same boy from my past, I glossed over our history instead. I tried to tell him, but I simply couldn't bring myself to do it.

"Yes, and I'm sorry for not bringing it up before. It was all work-related and I was distracted with the feature." Caleb and I were walking behind the others for some privacy on our way to the store. Caleb tried shrugging it off, but I could tell that he felt jealous. "As long as it was all related to the paper," he said.

"I mean, I haven't even been to your job, Clara. And

yet you invited him?"

I swallowed, feeling put on the spot. "You're right, I'm sorry I haven't had you come by yet. And yes, it was all about the paper."

"Alright then," he said calmly. We smiled at each other. "I'll go inside to get us a copy!" Ralph called out as he ran into the store. "*Get us a copy*, he says, as if I'm not getting my own copy of the paper that has the pictures that I took," Lauren said with an eye roll. "Yeah, and as if I'm not getting my own copy of the paper that has the feature that I wrote", I added with a laugh.

Ralph and Lauren returned shortly after, and we skimmed through the pages to get to my feature. Even though I'd read it over a hundred times, I still read over it religiously one more time. The pictures, all shot by Lauren, consisted of a closeup of the two thieves fighting with the old woman over the cash box, a wide shot of the thieves running away with it, then a closeup of one of the thieves on the ground, and lastly a closeup of Silas at the very end of his pitching motion. It was a miracle that Lauren was in the perfect position to photograph all of the action at that moment, but it was definitely more a demonstration of skill rather than just plain luck. Not only did she have the instinct to pull the camera up and photograph what was happening, but she did it flawlessly as none of the action was lost in her lens.

Wordlessly, I leaned into her as our eyes were still on the page. She reciprocates the gesture, and I knew that my appreciation for her reached her even without me saying it.

"You two, this came out great," Emmy said ecstatically. "It reads so professional, and Lauren, these photos. Wow!" Ralph whistled, his eyebrows raised. "I'm impressed. Passed my expectations, that's for sure."

I started to squirm internally, waiting to hear Caleb's opinion. Caleb's been waiting for me to get my shot at publishing a story, saying that editing didn't suit my style. I was hoping this could be the moment when he realized how serious this was for me, and that I might consider it as a career.

Caleb looked up from the page and gave me a soft kiss on the side of my head. "You killed it, Clara. I'm proud of you," he said sincerely. I looked up at him intending to give him a kiss, yet I stopped when I saw him looking at the feature again. His eyes looked frozen in time, and I realized he was staring at the closeup of Silas. "What a strange guy," he said with a deep breath.

"You weren't able to get him to try out for the team?" Ralph asked him.

"No shot at all. He said he only cares about himself, and yet he's ok with doing this and lets himself be interviewed and be added to the paper? Something just doesn't add up," he answered while shaking his head.

I started to feel irritated. Here I was, waiting for Caleb to give me my moment…and all he cared about and looked at was the photo of Silas? Also, what did he mean that something wasn't adding up? He's making it sound like it's against his character to have agreed to being interviewed, and that he only agreed to it because…

I looked up from the newspaper and stared out into the distance without focusing on anything specific.

He agreed to it because of me; because it was me that asked him to do it.

"It was my fault that I tripped, you know," Emmy piped up. "It was me that tripped over Mason. I was carrying some books, and I wasn't looking where I was going. His leg was stretched out; he didn't trip me on purpose."

"Mason's a jerk. Maybe he didn't trip you on purpose, but he didn't help you to pick your books up, right?" Ralph said up angrily. Emmy shrugged her shoulders sheepishly. "He was trying to tell me to be more careful and look where I was going. I'm sure he was going to start helping me right after. And yet at that same moment, Silas showed up. He didn't even hesitate to step in. He just got right up to Mason ready to stand up to him."

From the corner of my eye, I noticed Lauren suddenly brighten with an idea. I immediately started to worry, knowing that whenever an idea that popped into Lauren's head made her this happy, it was never a good sign.

I braced myself, but no amount of bracing could have prepared me for what she'd say next.

"Hey, we have plans to go to Mount Raven next month during that three-day weekend, right? We should invite him to ride the gondola with us!" Emmy's eyes widened with astonishment, and she started nodding profusely.

"Oh, I don't know…" I started to say, but Ralph cut me off. "You sure he'd agree to it? I mean, he didn't sound too enthusiastic when Caleb talked to him."

"He told me he wouldn't join the baseball team, not anything more than that. Maybe he'd agree to going to the gondola," Caleb answered, though he didn't look too enthusiastic about the idea. Lauren narrowed her eyes at him suspiciously. She looked about ready to tease him about Silas coming along, but I gave her an elbow to the side to shut her up.

"Come on, we need more guys to balance you the…you know, group," Emmy struggled to say. She was playing with her hair, a telltale sign that she was embarrassed. Ralph and Caleb gave each other helpless looks.

I rolled my head backwards, defeated. My goal wasn't to exclude Silas, but to avoid having him and Caleb in the same place. I was trying to stop Caleb from realizing who Silas was.

"You know him the best since you interviewed him, Clara. You mind inviting him?" Lauren asked me. I looked over at her, shocked. I saw a mischievous look in her eye that forced me to swallow.

Everyone in the group was suddenly staring at me, waiting for me to agree. I sighed, putting up the most passive face I could muster.

"Sure, I'll talk to him. No guarantees he'll agree to it, though."

***

Two weeks went by, and I still hadn't asked Silas about Mount Raven. I could have gone out of my way to ask him by going to his house, but something kept holding me back. I had started finding it difficult to imagine myself sitting in a gondola with both Caleb and Silas at the same time. The idea alone caused me to procrastinate, even though I'm not entirely sure what his answer would be in the first place.

I was sitting alone on the bleachers by the baseball field, waiting for Caleb to finish up his practice. He offered to drive me to work when he was done, so I brought some work to do some editing while I waited.

Feeling distracted, I fished out my copy of the local paper that I shoved into my schoolbag. I thought I was weird for carrying it with me everywhere, but Lauren had done the same thing, which made me feel better since it meant that I wasn't the only one.

I read over the feature again, mulling over the quote that I got from Silas.

If you're going to report on the attempted theft at the market, you should highlight the increase in crime that's been happening in this town, Silas had said.

What increase in crime? I couldn't help but ask myself. Silas's one isolated incident at that gas station and his other fight the day he came home with bloodied teeth couldn't mean there was an increase in crime throughout the entire town, could it?

Leaning back on the bleachers, I thought back to things I'd been hearing from my coworkers. For some inexplicable reason, our office begin assigning a small task force dedicated solely to reporting local crime, but

I heard these crimes were small and non-threatening. The crimes were small and petty, which was why the curfew had been put in place targeting those that were underage. Silas had to have been wrong about the town.

Right?

I scanned the field, knowing that practice should be coming to an end soon. I saw something in passing before looking back down to the page on my lap. Once my brain processed what my eyes had seen, my head jerked upwards as I looked to the field again.

Silas was approaching the field with a neutral expression on his face. If he had seen me sitting on the bleachers, he didn't make it obvious. I put all of the work I brought with me and my copy of the paper back into my bag in a rush. I meandered over to where the other boys were huddled around to hear what was going on.

Fall River's baseball coach was addressing all of the boys. I gave Caleb a shy wave when our eyes met, and he gave me an apprehensive look. I discreetly moved my head around to see Silas standing on the pitcher's mound, warming up his pitching arm.

When the group disbanded, Caleb jogged over to me and planted a quick kiss on my cheek.

"Sorry, Clara, I need a few more minutes before I can take you to work."

"It's ok, don't worry about that. What's going on here? Why is Silas…" I trailed off, looking at the boys all starting to huddle around home plate.

"I just can't understand that guy," Caleb answered

as he looked over at Silas. "He spoke to the coach. He's issuing our team a challenge. Everyone gets one at-bat against him. If anyone manages to get a hit on him, then he said he'd consider joining the team."

Caleb scoffed loudly. "Who does he think he is? What's worse, the coach is taking the challenge seriously. He said to do our best and try to get a hit no matter what. If this is his way of trying out for our team—"

"He's not trying out for the team," the coach said in passing as he overheard us. He recognized me as Caleb's girlfriend, and he gave me a smile. "Think if it as the team trying out for him."

I could tell the comment bothered Caleb from the loud *tsk* he made as he turned and headed towards the other boys on the home plate.

"Were you trying to light a fire under his feet?" I asked the coach, trying to see what his angle was. The coach didn't break eye contact with his boys. "There's no guarantee that Silas sticks around even after this. But I would never turn down the opportunity to give my team some additional experience."

The coach exhaled loudly, and I looked over at him curiously. "Especially," the coach emphasized,

"...From a pitcher like that."

Just when I started to wonder who was going to take to the batter's box first, one boy volunteered before anyone else.

"I'll go first! Prepare to join our team, Silas!"

Ralph's loud declaration was bold, and I noticed a smirk on Silas's face.

"What was the challenge, exactly?" I asked the coach.

"Silas claimed no one on the team would get a hit on him at all," he laughed. "I talked him out of that and modified the challenge to make it that no one can get a good hit on him; foul balls not included."

Ralph smiled confidently as he got into his batting position. Fall River's catcher was already in position behind him. I couldn't help but notice the stark contrast of the sight; Ralph and the catcher in Fall River's uniform while Silas was wearing casual clothes. There wasn't even a glove in his hand.

Silas prepared to pitch—

Boom!

The sound was the only indicator that a ball had even been thrown. Ralph hadn't moved an inch, his bat frozen in the exact same place in the air. All of the confidence Ralph had only moments earlier was long gone.

"I…I couldn't even see it," Ralph said, sounding deeply impressed.

I looked over at the catcher that had Silas's ball in his glove. My eyes were drawn to the ball, and I could see the almost imperceptible shaking of the catchers' hand beneath that glove.

Without a word, the catcher stood up and looked around. Clearly the person he was looking for was the coach, because his eyes stopped looking around when he saw him. The coach knew exactly what he was looking around for.

"I brought a backup one from the dugout! Go

ahead and switch it out!"

The catcher nodded, jogging over to the dugout. The other boys looked at him nervously, and I could see Caleb refuse to break eye contact with Silas.

"What's going on?" I asked. "That ball was probably among the fastest our catcher has ever caught in his glove," the coach answered calmly. "If he's going to last long enough to catch more than a few pitches from that pitcher, he's going to need a glove that's at its maximum potential."

"Also, if you haven't noticed," the coach continued. "That pitcher isn't even warmed up. That was his first pitch…cold."

I stared as the catcher continued his way to the dugout, his hand still trembling from the impact of Silas's powerful first pitch.

After Ralph was struck out, the rest of the Fall River team continued to drop like flies against Silas's pitches. It was difficult to picture anyone standing up to the speed and technique that Silas was capable of. As more and more batters approached the challenge, I began to understand exactly why the coach was so accepting of Silas's wager.

The Fall River batters became demoralized with every effortless strikeout. It looked as if the confidence of each batter continued to dwindle with each passing player. I looked over to the coach to gauge his reaction, but he seemed unphased. I got the idea that the coach wasn't just trying to give the team an opportunity to bat against a pitcher like Silas, but also to get them to work on their mental fortitude.

In no time at all, there was only one batter left to take to home plate: Caleb.

Leading up to his turn, Caleb started to perform practice swings beside the other players with a weighted ring that sat almost halfway up on the bat. Even though it wasn't his turn, I could hear the strong swings from Caleb's bat from where the coach and I were standing.

My stomach was in knots with the thought of the two boys facing off against each other. On one hand, I couldn't help but stare at Silas's incredible ability. It wasn't the abilities of a boy who was coasting and taking advantage of his innate skill; he had obviously been practicing.

With every pitch, I saw flashes of the young boy I knew was a prodigy and used to see pitching in the park near our house. Even though his form had been perfected, I could still manage to make out the younger him mirroring the same precise movements.

On the other hand, it was becoming almost impossible to overlook the unbearable overconfidence that Silas was displaying on the pitcher's mound. As more players were struck out, he started to yawn and pretended to look bored. It was enough to make me want to walk over to him and tell him off; this was his challenge to the Fall River boys, not the other way around. How did he get off trying to show off and make everyone feel bad? Who was he even showing off to?

Finally, Caleb approached the batter's box. He slammed the heel of his bat on the ground, causing the round weight to fall over the handle and fall to the ground. He leveled his eyes at Silas, looking unflinchingly at his bored-looking face.

Just as he was starting to get ready to pitch, Silas looked over at me for the first time. My breath caught as we made eye-contact, especially since I wasn't expecting him to wink at me.

"Any thoughts on how this will go?" the coach asked.

"I'm honestly not sure…" I answered, feeling somewhat distracted after Silas's overconfident wink.

"You're not sure?" the coach asked, sounding surprised. "If you really don't know how this will go, then you haven't been paying enough attention to that boyfriend of yours."

Before I could open my mouth to ask what he meant, Silas made his first pitch. Caleb's face was hardened, and his bat moved at an impressive speed—

Clink!

I watched, bewildered, as the ball flew out into the distance. The ball had flown off to the side, way outside of the foul line.

My eyes were immediately drawn to Caleb right afterwards, and I could see a bright and relaxed smile on his face. It was a look that seemed as if he had figured something out, or that things just suddenly made sense. Without wasting any time, Caleb raised his bat and looked ready for the next pitch. It was clearly a challenge of his own to Silas, daring him to pitch at him again.

Silas suddenly looked like an entirely different

person in that moment. The bored, absent look in his eyes was replaced with one of true stoicism.

I felt a strange sensation in my chest seeing them both looking at each other so intensely. I felt like I was looking at the beginning of a new rivalry, one that would last as long as either of them could still hold a baseball and bat, respectively.

Crack!

Caleb's second swing connected, yet it landed outside of the foul line once again. Silas's eyes never left the ball as it flew through the air even faster than the previous one. The two balls curved at the end, and yet it was no match for Caleb; his bat made its way to the ball with ease.

A smile crept onto my face as I looked at Caleb. His easygoing smile was infectious, and I knew he was thrilled at the challenge. He looked hungry, like he could continue batting until he keeled over from exhaustion. Silas, on the other hand, looked rigid and uneasy. Unlike Caleb, he didn't look like he was having any fun. Silas seemed as if he truly had something to lose if Caleb beat him, even though he said he would just consider joining if he lost.

Why do you seem so troubled, Silas? I couldn't help but ask myself.

Ping!

I didn't have to follow the ball to know that its trajectory was fair game. The ball flew straight over Silas's head at a breakneck speed. In fact, it wouldn't have surprised me if the ball was a homerun.

Silas didn't waste any time; he gathered the things

he laid around himself and started walking straight out of the field. He never looked over to Caleb or me again, yet he had to walk in my direction in order to leave the field.

"What Silas was missing," the coach spoke up resolutely. "Was someone capable to meet his level and rise to the challenge. Caleb was the perfect person to do that."

I looked over at the coach trying to understand.

"You see, it's easy to become complacent when you win games with ease."

The coach started to walk towards the boys as they huddled around Caleb excitedly, cheering on his victory. Caleb looked happy, and amidst all the commotion, he looked through it all and sought me out. When our eyes met, he gave me a deeply warm and prideful smile. It was a smile that I couldn't help but return.

"For players like Silas, having someone force you out of your comfort zone is the only true way to push past your limits and swallow your pride enough to accept the true feeling of defeat."

Silas walked past me without a second look, his eyes stuck on the ground. I was so distracted watching him walk away that I completely missed Caleb jogging up next to me and planting another kiss on my cheek.

"Silas, hey," Caleb called out before he got too far away. He stood beside me and looked at Silas with a determined smile. Despite looking as if he would like nothing more than to ignore him, Silas turned to face us.

"Seems to me that you play baseball to win, and nothing else," Caleb said. "There are other reasons to play baseball, you know. Like playing on a team and helping those around you grow."

Caleb exhaled loudly from his nose. "That's why you lost today, Silas. You came here to show off while I was here to help my team win. We are worlds apart."

Silas didn't react right away. After a couple of moments, Silas scoffed loudly.

"Sounds troublesome," is all he said before turning away.

6

"Sweetheart, how about I'll do the rooms, and you do the rest?"

"Long as you do the bathrooms, too."

"Hmm. You make lunch for today, then."

"That's a deal."

It's Sunday, the day my mother designated as the weekly cleaning day. I usually complained about it but this week things are different; I'm thankful for the distraction. My mind kept going in circles about my feature and the implications of what Silas told me. On top of that, I just couldn't manage to keep Silas out of my mind, either.

As if he had thrown a wrench in my brain, I just couldn't stop thinking about my visit to his room, his visit to my job, and of course his face-off against Caleb. Caleb himself didn't talk much about the challenge or Silas at all, which I was thankful for. Anything I could do to try to get my mind on anything that wasn't Silas, I was more than happy to do.

I was mindlessly pondering over Silas when a knock on the door caught my attention.

"Someone's at the door, mom!" I called out. "Make sure it's not strangers!" she called back.

I looked through the peephole and went rigid. "Oh, they're definitely strangers, mom."

"What?" I heard her footsteps approaching but opened the door anyway, knowing there wasn't going to be any avoiding it.

"Good morning, might you be Clara?" one of the two police officers in front of the doorway asked me. I nodded silently. "Nice to meet you. My partner and I are detectives. Mind if we come in for a few questions? Shouldn't take long."

"My daughter in any trouble?" my mother asked gravely. "None at all, please don't worry," the second detective clarified. "In fact, we're hoping she could help us out with an ongoing investigation we have."

We all sat on one of the two couches in the living room. My mother and I sat on one and the detectives on the other across from us. I started feeling nervous, wondering if my feature broke the law of some sort. The detectives were about to start explaining what was going on when another knock interrupted them.

"Clara, you in there?"

The sound of Silas's voice made my heartbeat quicken tremendously. I got right to my feet and opened the door to see Silas panting on the other side of the door. He looked at me with an almost desperate expression. Silas's entire behavior changed when his eyes met mine. As soon as that happened, he made a deep sigh of relief.

"You alright?" he asked quietly.

"Uh-huh," I said awkwardly.

"There's a police car in front of your house—"

"I can see it, Silas."

"There usually isn't one there, you know—"

"I know there usually isn't a police car in front of my house, Silas."

"I thought something had happened to you—"

"Thank you," I breathed. I smiled nervously at him. His concern for me was completely unexpected, yet it made me elated. He must have sprinted over here as fast as he could when he saw the police cruiser outside.

"Er, you wouldn't happen to be Silas, would you?" one of the detectives asked awkwardly. He was craning his neck to look at us from the couch.

"Mind if I come inside, Clara?" Silas asked me. I nodded, moving to the side to give him space to come inside.

Silas waited for me to sit on the couch before sitting between my mother and me. It might have been my imagination, but as soon as he sat down, Silas inched himself just slightly closer to me.

"Yes, that's me," Silas addressed the detectives. "If this has anything to do with Clara's feature, then I'd like to hear about it because I was also present."

Silas's confidence had a reassuring effect on me. I was sure that Silas had my back. I looked at the detectives again, feeling leagues calmer than I felt just moments before.

"That's great because we were going to come to visit you next," the detective informed us. "This does have to do with the story that was published in the local newspaper earlier this week, the one that involved the theft."

"Everything was reported to the authorities. Cops arrived at the scene. And Caleb—my boyfriend—he chased after the vehicle and called in where he last saw it."

"Yes, we know all of that. The story and your testimony were great assets in our investigation. It's because of that we're here now." I stared at the investigators blankly. Silas nudged me in the shoulder suddenly, making me flustered by how close he was sitting next to me.

"The case went cold, *Ms. Reporter.* They're hoping we could help them," Silas whispered into my ear coyly.

"Ah, that's certainly a way to put it," one of the detectives said as they gave each other a look. "We're hoping you have anything else you might have left out from your report and story. Is there anything that comes to mind?"

I looked over to Silas. "Tell them about the gas station." Silas looked back at me, somewhat unsettled. He doesn't argue, though, and told the detectives about the fight he had against the three man that were trying to rob the young couple with the baby in the car.

"Thank you, yes we are well aware of that fight," one of the detectives answered.

"Speaking of fights, Silas," the other detective said as he shifted on the couch. "We know about another incident you got into earlier this month. Care to explain what that fight was about?"

I sat up straighter on the couch. That's right, Silas had told me about his fight at the gas station, not the fight he had when he came home with blood-stained teeth.

I sneaked a peek over at him, hoping he would spill the beans. He and I made eye contact again, and he immediately closed them before sighing deeply towards the ground. I was starting to notice that Silas had the inexplicable inability to turn me down when it came to me asking things of him. I knew that he couldn't refuse telling the story once I asked, so he gave in and was going to tell it.

"I was in a general store near here and there was a creep groping a woman. He cornered her and was feeling her up. She was uncomfortable with it, so I stepped in. Things got physical." The investigators scoffed. "That creep was a repeat offender and a notorious fighter in prison."

"Yeah, and it wasn't hard to find him after his fight with you. We just followed the trail of blood he left before passing out behind the store."

I blinked at the investigators in astonishment. "That's quite the ability you have, Silas," the investigators said in agreement.

"Gentlemen, please, do not encourage his behavior," my mom pleaded. The investigators coughed, trying to get serious again. "Is there anything more you can tell us about what you've seen? Perhaps there's something that links the two fights you got into? We're trying to find something on the criminal that got away from the farmer's market."

Silas got quiet, mulling it over in his head. He spoke up after a beat.

"Wait, now that I think about it, there was something…"

Silas got to his feet. He looked over at me, his brow furrowed as he contemplated something. "Clara, can you bring me your copy of the paper your feature is in?" My shoulders jerked upwards slightly at hearing him call out my name so earnestly. "Right, I'll bring it right now," I answered, heading to my room to bring the copy I had inside my school bag.

I brought it to the living room and handed it to Silas, who opened the paper and laid it flat on the short coffee table between the two couches. Silas didn't have to flip through the paper; he knew exactly where my feature was. He stared at the different photographs, and his eyes froze as he looked at the closeup of the two thieves.

"Here. The thief that got away, he had a tattoo on his left forearm. I saw that same tattoo on the guys I fought at the gas station, and the creep from the store. They all had that tattoo."

The investigators leaned over the image possessively. "Yeah…yeah the creep does have that tattoo, I remember that." The other officer got up, deep in thought.

"You two have been a great help. If we have any

more questions, we will make sure to reach out." My mother and I walked the investigators to the door and closed it before finally relaxing.

I didn't relax for long, though, since Silas was currently sitting comfortably on the couch in my living room.

I walked over to him, trying to come up with something to say. And yet, it seems that wasn't necessary. "Ms. Monroe, do you mind if I talk with Clara for a moment? There's something I want to ask her about."

My mother looked troubled as she stared at the door long after the officers left. "Yes, please go ahead. I'm going to go and talk with your mother to calm my nerves. Is she home?"

"She was the one that told me about the police car outside. She'll be wanting to hear what happened, too."

What used to make me nervous about Silas being in my living room now made me nervous that Silas was in my *actual* room. I couldn't be more thankful that I cleaned my own room just before moving to the rest of the house. Silas made his way into my room and sat on my office chair, seemingly unbothered. I walked mechanically over to my schoolbag and was about to put away the paper when Silas asked me for it. He started to stare at the feature again.

While he analyzed the feature again, I walked over to my bed and sat down at the very edge of it, closest to him.

"What did you think?" he asked, serious.

"I think that you're right. The case went cold on

them. I mean, it has to be if they got desperate enough to ask a couple of highschoolers what else they might know."

Silas gave me a look over the top of the newspaper. "You're not 'just a highschooler', you know. You work for the paper. You're a reporter—a journalist."

I made a face at the comment. Even though I managed to report on and publish my own feature, I still didn't feel like a genuine reporter. I felt like someone who got lucky and was handed the opportunity on a silver platter.

That's right. I wasn't a reporter, I was just someone who got lucky, was all.

"Clara, tell me what you make of this," Silas asked as he showed me the feature again, his finger on top of the tattoo. Even though I'd seen it a hundred times, I looked at the image closely again.

"I really don't know, Silas."

Silas leaned back on his chair, looking frustrated. "I wish we had a better image of it."

I brightened up at the comment. "Lauren. She took the photos. I think one of the ones she took might show the tattoo better than the ones I used on the feature."

I had clearly captured Silas's attention. He leaned forward on the chair and opened his mouth, about to ask about seeing them as soon as possible.

That was my moment to strike.

"My friends want you to come to Mount Raven with us; to ride the gondola." My heart felt like it was beating out of my chest. Silas closed his mouth, waiting for me to continue.

"I can ask Lauren to bring some printed photos of the tattoos so we can look at them together when we meet up at Mount Raven."

"What is it that you want, Clara?"

I blinked at him profusely, the question leaving me winded. Silas leaned slightly closer to me, closing the distance between us painstakingly slowly.

"I—I want you to come too," I answered, feeling like a stammering mess.

Silas stopped his slow approach, his eyes fixed on the ground by my feet. Something seemed to catch his attention, yet my eyes didn't have the ability to look away from him in the slightest.

"I'll ride my bike there," is all he said.

Silas then headed for the door. "Tell Lauren about the photos," he instructed as he walked. I meant to ask him what was up with his obsession over the tattoo, but Silas was long gone before I managed to get my thoughts in order again.

Curious about what Silas was looking at, I looked down at my feet. I realized, horrified, that my shoebox with girly stickers was peeking out from under my bed just enough for it to have been visible from where Silas was sitting.

There's no way he'd remember…

I tried to convince myself as I stared at the box.

And yet I knew there was no use in doubting it. Silas definitely remembered the shoebox as the special place I used to store the keepsakes he'd given me before he moved away.

7

"Clara!"

I looked over my shoulder to see Lauren approaching, and I waved at her nervously. Her look of excitement was a stark contrast from the strange turmoil I had in my heart.

"Ready to get our investigative hats on?" she asked. I nodded at her and turned to face the building in front of us.

It's the weekend, and after the police investigators visited my house to question me about my feature, I wanted to dig deeper to read about other crimes that have been happening in Fall River.

Were the fights that Silas has gotten into truly isolated incidents? I wanted to know. *Is the curfew truly about petty crimes like graffiti, and nothing more?*

I swallowed, hard. *Are there more crimes we don't know about?*

I asked Lauren to meet up with me in front of the Fall River Public Library, the only one in town.

"Before we go in, there's something I need to ask you," I asked her. She looked over at me expectantly.

"Did…police investigators come to your house in the past few days?"

The single strap bag Lauren had brought with her slid down her shoulder and fell straight to the ground. Her face was scrunched up in shock.

"I'll take that as a no," I said with a quiet exhale. "Clara, what do you mean investigators?"

"They came to ask me about the case on the thief from the farmer's market. The case went cold on them, and they wanted to know if I had any more information."

I made a face as I looked at Lauren. "I suspected they would visit you too since you were the photographer behind the pictures in my feature but looks like I was wrong."

"That's why you asked me to comb through the old editions about the crimes that have been happening in town?"

I nodded in reply.

Searching through old newspapers would've been too difficult alone, so I asked Lauren to come with me. Past editions were kept on file in bound volumes, so I had no worries that I'd be missing anything.

"Let's get to work then," Lauren said resolutely as she walked towards the entrance to the library before me. I smiled after her in appreciation.

"Clara, why didn't you just ask your coworkers for

the old features the local paper has written? Wouldn't that be more direct instead of searching what you need in here, blind?" Lauren asked as she and I were combing through the old editions.

"For some reason, when I asked them, I got some strange looks from the editors at the paper." I furrowed my brow. "They gave me strange excuses about why they couldn't help me, making it clear that I should drop it."

"Huh, weird," she said. "Trust me, I know."

"You can count on me. We'll find something," Lauren answered. I knew I could count on Lauren's help. I returned my focus on the bounded editions I had in front of me and got back to work.

"Doing research with you is great, Clara," Lauren sighed after an hour of browsing through old newspapers. I blinked at her and grinned.

"You think we'll be able to keep working like this? I mean in journalism; me behind the camera, and you doing the interviews and writing the stories?"

I could tell by the tone of her voice that she was desperate, holding on to a small ray of hope. I extended a hand and placed it on her hand that was laid on the bench between us.

"I wouldn't have it any other way," I answered wholeheartedly. "There isn't a photographer in the world that I'd trust my story to than you, Lauren."

Lauren dropped her chin down to her chest, looking like I'd just told her she won the lottery.

"I never told you how happy it makes me to have you count on me," she said quietly. "So, please…"

She paused, giving me a confident look in her eyes.

"Trust me, I'll be there for you when you need me."

Her seriousness took me by surprise. I gave her a delighted look as she moved her hand to be on top of mine and gave it a squeeze.

"On that note, I think I found something interesting," Lauren said as she started to stretch. "Give this a look."

I scooted over to where she was and eyed the edition she had in front of her.

The paper covered a kidnapping that happened in Fall River, the first kidnapping this town had seen in over forty years. In a town this small, a kidnapping like that was unheard of. Everyone knew each other, and news like this would have reached every household in a matter of days.

A hand shot up to my mouth, shocked. "What? I never heard about this anywhere—"

"Look here," Lauren said, pointing a reserved finger up to the top where the date was.

I held up the faded, distinct page. "This date…I know exactly what stories were printed that date. It looks like the right paper, so why does the library have this page? This doesn't seem real…"

"I don't know how the library even gets the paper. How does that work?" Lauren asked.

"Wait a minute," I breathed. I felt the thin, slightly better-quality paper. "It *is* real, almost. Before presses are run, editors get a final proof, a clean advance copy of the paper's layout, to give it the last official sign-off. It's the last step before mass production."

"An advance copy?" Lauren asked. She got the paper from me and flipped it over to see the blank back. "So, they filed it here by mistake?"

"Exactly," I answered, working things out in my head. "This story had to have been killed *just* before the paper was hitting the press. They must have swapped it with another story instead. Someone in circulation had already dropped this proof in the bin destined for the library archive. They filed the copy before the official print run had even started. This page is what the paper *intended* to publish."

"Who could have intervened to stop the story so late into the printing process?" Lauren asked.

I looked at the date the story had and Silas's voice came to mind.

And since when is there a curfew here? Everyone under the age of 21 has to be indoors before 8 PM? When was that implemented? What's the deal with that?

"The girl that was kidnapped was underage and happened at the same time that the curfew made by the police was put in place."

"You think the police are covering this story up? They were the ones that intervened on the story?" She looked down at the page again. "That would explain the curfew. I always thought doing a curfew over graffiti and noise complaints was a strange move."

I read the entire contents of the paper. "The girl was found, safe and alive. But the kidnapper is still on the run."

"Is this something along the lines of what you were looking for?" Lauren asked, hopeful.

I reached over and gave her a quick embrace as a reply. "You don't know the start of it," I answered. "I owe you a coffee, Lauren."

She gave me a triumphant glance. "Make it a coffee and dessert and I'll be the happiest girl in the world."

I thought of Silas at that moment and remembered the photos of the tattoo from the farmer's market he wanted to see.

"Lauren, there's another small favor I need to ask you…"

***

Silas's mother, my mother, and I were all sitting in Silas's living room, looking over a photo album of Silas and I when we were younger. How I ended up getting dragged into this, I didn't even remember. These pictures of Silas filled my brain, exactly as I remembered him from my youth.

"Remember how he used to go over to your house and ask if Clara was free to play?" Lisette asked. "Oh, like it was yesterday," my mom replied. One set of pictures caught my eye, and I pointed them out. "When were these from?"

"Hm, remember this day, Davie?" Lisette asked with a knowing smile. "Last New Years before Silas left, 1992, wasn't it?" my mom answered. Lisette didn't respond, just nodded as her eyes never left the photo.

I tried my best to remember anything from that day, and yet my memory kept drawing a blank. The photos were taken at a park I recognized near our house, so our families must have made plans to spend New Years there. Instinctively, I reached out to the pictures and placed a finger over young Silas.

"Hey, is this where Silas got his obsession over motorcycles?" I asked, seeing a photo of a little Silas and I staring at a bike. There was a guy on the bike, and he was looking at the camera. I must've missed a joke because Lisette and my mom started bursting out, laughing.

"Look closer, honey," my mom managed between breaths. "It's you that's into the bike." Perplexed, I looked at the picture again. I could see that my eyes were fixated on the biker on the motorcycle.

"Have I…always been into biker guys?" I asked with a deadpan expression. "And if you look even closer," Lisette said as she pointed out Silas in the picture.

"Someone looks like he's noticed your interest in them." I looked at little Silas, who was looking at me with a slightly pouting, seemingly jealous face. It was a timeless face that I couldn't have been more disappointed to have missed in person, and yet was infinitely happier that it was captured in a photograph.

8

A strong breeze caught my attention and brought my gaze to Mount Raven in the distance. Most of our group had gathered at the base of the gondola, the large cables right above us. The only two people missing were Emmy, and the newest addition: Silas.

I pulled Lauren aside of the others so that we could talk away from the other guys. "You brought the photos, right?" I asked her.

"Sure did. I brought the pictures where the tattoo looked the clearest."

I nodded, prepared to rejoin the others, but Lauren grabbed my arm. "You think everything is related, don't you? Even the research we did in the library, right?"

"I suspect so," I answered. "Let's wait until things settle down. We'll tell the entire group at once."

"You absolutely made the right choice telling your

best friend first. If you'd told me at the same time as everyone else, I'd have disowned you."

I laughed and gave her a playful eyeroll before turning away and walking back to Caleb and Ralph.

"Wait, did Emmy ever say how she was getting here?" Ralph asked. I rode here with Caleb, and Lauren caught a ride with Ralph, something I was sure he was ecstatic about. "No, I don't think she ever said," I answered.

A motorcycle approached the parking lot in front of the ski lift. I recognized the bike as Silas's, and the conversation I had with my mom and Lisette regarding how he noticed my interest in biker guys repeated itself in my head.

"Oh, so that was how she caught a ride!" Lauren exclaimed. Silas turned a corner and for the first time I saw someone behind him.

The person sitting behind him was holding onto Silas tightly around his waist. I felt a plummeting feeling in my stomach and couldn't look away. I watched as Silas parked his bike, waiting patiently for the girl to step off before dismounting himself. The girl had a helmet on, and so did he. I wasn't sure that it was Emmy until Silas helped her get her helmet off and I saw her timid face pop out from underneath it. Her cheeks reddened as she looked up at Silas, who took his own helmet off effortlessly. Silas reached over and removed a cap, which he placed on his head.

As the pair approached us, Emmy gave Lauren and I a silent, wide-eyed stare with tight lips. "Oh, I'm going to need to hear all about this," Lauren whispered to me in the ear. I looked at Silas, trying to gauge his reaction, but our eyes didn't meet even once. It felt like he was purposefully avoiding my gaze. I looked at his head and noticed his cap; it was the same one I had said looked good on him, the one from his desk.

Silas approached quietly, and I recalled the challenge he made against the Fall River team. I looked over to the Caleb and Ralph and could tell that they were waiting to see exactly how Silas would act before saying anything themselves.

It looked as if he could tell what they were thinking, because Silas gave them an amused look. He extended a calm fist and held it in front of himself in the air. Caleb and Ralph smiled before bumping Silas's fist. The gesture was over quickly, but I could tell that there was a new sense of respect between them, especially on Silas's part.

"Sorry we're late, I was taking forever to decide my outfit, so…" Emmy said meekly. "I also got a little turned around trying to find the right house," Silas added. "Yeah, you weren't even close," Emmy joked. She had a shy smile, and her fingers were playing with the bottom of her jacket.

Silas and Emmy shared a quick, quiet laugh. The sight made me feel a lump in my throat, and an inexplicable pain in my chest started to build. I caught Caleb and Ralph sharing a look, and Lauren hooked her arm through mine suddenly.

"Shall we get going, then?" Lauren asked. I glanced over at Silas and felt a chill. His eyes were fixed, absolutely locked on my left hand. I followed his gaze and realized the only thing my left hand was doing was lacing its fingers through Caleb's. Lauren started pulling me along, and I let go of Caleb's hand without meaning to.

"They sure looked comfortable, right?" Lauren told me as we led the group through the line to get to the gondola. I snuck a glance at Silas and Emmy, who were at the back. Emmy's quiet, but she kept sneaking glances at Silas while he stared at the gondola, transfixed. "Did Emmy ever mention liking Silas?" I asked.

"Hard to not fall for a guy who stood up for you at the drop of a hat," Lauren answered, referring to when she fell after walking into Mason. "Looks like you took too long to scoop him up." I shot her a look. "Question is whether Silas likes her back." She placed extra emphasis on the question, which started to gnaw at me. I didn't want to feel this way, whatever this feeling was. If Emmy liked a boy, I always wanted to support her, same went for Lauren. And yet…

For a reason I couldn't explain, I just couldn't right now.

We all approached the ticket booth, and Caleb paid for my ticket. Ralph offered to pay for Lauren's ticket, but she refused. I snuck a glance behind me and watched as Silas paid for his ticket and Emmy's without even getting her input. She gave Silas a look of quiet admiration as he handed her the ticket wordlessly.

Once we got to the front of the gondola line, an employee told us something that halted us all in our tracks.

"It's five people maximum per cabin," he said dryly. So, you'll have to split up."

The world started spinning as I realized that Emmy and Silas might ride alone, meaning they'd be in that enclosed space for about ten minutes. I stiffened up and turned around as quickly as I could, trying to suggest the idea of splitting up into two equal groups before anyone else said anything. That's when I saw Emmy looking up at Silas expectantly, as if she was waiting for his reply. I just knew she had already asked him if he wanted to ride alone with her.

"You should ride with your friends," I caught Silas saying after a beat. "Besides, I've never ridden on one of these before. I sort of want to enjoy it alone the first time."

I felt the air I had been holding in my lungs hiss from behind my teeth. Everyone filled in the bright red gondola, leaving Silas behind. I looked through the window back at him, hoping he couldn't see me staring at him. Silas didn't return the look; he simply waited for the next gondola with a vacant expression.

"Did you see his bike? It looked sick," Ralph told Caleb. "I didn't know he liked to ride motorcycles." I gave him a look. "I literally told you he rode bikes," I answered. "Yeah, I thought you meant he rode a bicycle everywhere, not that he had a sportsbike."

"I'd prefer my Mustang, but that really was a cool bike," Caleb added. "I just wouldn't ride one. Too dangerous, you know? Even in a small town."

"He ever talk about that challenge again?" Ralph

asked. Caleb looked out the window beside him. "Never did, just like I thought he would. I'm glad I was able to put him in his place. I'll be ready in case he ever wants to challenge me—us—again."

"I was really hoping he'd join after you got that hit—"

"Enough about bikes and challenges! I want to hear about you and Silas. Spill it! You asked him for a ride, and he agreed?" Lauren asked desperately, as if containing the question for even a second longer would cause her to explode. Emmy seemed to shrink into the seat beneath her. "Well, yeah, I asked him. He agreed right away, it was fun to ride behind him. He's a gentleman."

Lauren snapped her fingers loudly. "He's a hottie and he's a gentleman? Two-for-two."

Ralph and Caleb tensed up, as if they had to say something to counterbalance the compliments Silas was being given.

"Well, there's his reclusive nature. He turned down riding with anyone on the gondola and clearly doesn't like to play baseball on a team," Ralph listed out.

"There's also that aggression and sense of superiority he has," Caleb said nonchalantly.

I let out a loud laugh. "C'mon you guys, jealous much?" I asked looking over at them. They squirmed in their seats, clearly fretting over being called out.

"If I'm being honest, though," Emmy said reluctantly. "I really don't think he likes me. He's been really nice, but I don't think he means anything about it. He's just friendly."

"He bought your ticket for you," Ralph said. "That's got to mean something, right?" I rolled my eyes at him, seeing clear as day that Ralph is desperate to be sure that Silas liked Emmy so that Lauren wouldn't go after him herself.

"I'm glad you two seem to be getting together. I was starting to think he had a thing for Clara," Caleb said nonchalantly.

In the next moment, the gondola stopped moving, leaving us suspended in the air, yet I hardly even noticed. Caleb had just caused my brain to short-circuit.

"You…what?" I said under my breath.

"You noticed that too? I wasn't going to say anything," Ralph said with a slap on his knee.

"What are you guys talking about?" Lauren asked. She looked nonchalant, but I knew it took every ounce of her being to keep her excitement under wraps. Emmy gave the boys a curious look, clearly interested in hearing the answer as well.

"Hm, it's a guy thing I guess," Ralph said after a beat. "Hard to explain, but we just get an idea when a guy likes a girl."

"Hard to explain to a *girl*, you mean?" I asked with one of my eyebrows raised.

"It's like we have this built-in radar that tips us off when a guy is interested in a girl, you know?" Ralph struggled to explain.

"If only you had one of those for when girls like you, not one for guys," Emmy laughed.

"I wouldn't explain it like that, Ralph—" Caleb said,

but it was too late. The entire gondola erupted into a fit of hysterics.

"Good to know that you boys have a radar for *guys*," Lauren managed to say between gasps for air.

Tried as I might to join in on the laughter, I couldn't get over what Caleb and Ralph said.

What if there was some truth to what they were saying? I asked myself.

The air in the cabin was light and lively. The sound of the low, mechanical drone of the cable overhead was loud but barely heard over the laughter. With a subtle lurch, the gondola began its slow, inevitable crawl upward. I stared determinedly out the window, watching the trees as we rose.

9

We waited for Silas to exit his gondola by the platform. As he got off, he had a quick exchange with the employee that oversaw making sure everyone exited safely. He joined us shortly after. I was about to open my mouth to ask what that was about when Emmy beat me to the question.

"Do you know him?" she asked sweetly, leaning into Silas slightly. My eyes widened as I saw Silas place a comforting hand on Emmy's back as he answered. "There was a lost pair of gloves in my cabin. I was handing it to the employee."

I saw Emmy's shoulders quiver slightly as Silas's hand made contact with her back. I clenched my right fist and turned away, trying to erase the sight from my memory. Ralph's next suggestion helped significantly.

"Guys, I'm starving, let's make a quick stop at Cliff Point before going to the spot," he said as he led the way.

There's a sole restaurant atop Mount Raven known as Cliff Point, and we all filtered in.

"I told him to eat something before coming for this reason," Lauren said with an eye roll, causing Emmy and I to snicker.

We barely made it into the restaurant when we saw a familiar face.

"Wait, is that Mason?" Lauren nearly squawked. Mason looked over at our group from the table he was waiting on. I had to do a double take upon seeing him. He looked surprisingly good in a waiter uniform. After he finished writing someone's order on a notepad, he approached us, though his eyes were almost exclusively focused on only one person in our group.

"You're here?" he directed at Lauren with a look of genuine surprise on his face. "Hey, we're here too…" Ralph trailed off. Mason looked at the rest of us for seemingly the first time.

"Oh, right," Mason said.

"What, you here to trip customers and spill people's drinks on them?" Lauren huffed.

Mason made a hurt expression. "That was an accident." Lauren made a *hmph* sound and linked her arm through Emmy's. "C'mon," she said as she pushed through deeper into the restaurant.

I looked after them and remembered how Mason and Silas almost got into a fight the last time they saw each other. I turned to see them and noticed some sparks going off as they made eye contact.

"You're not going to fight, right guys?" I asked

softly. At the question, Mason and Silas nodded at each other at almost the same exact time. A sign of mutual respect, if I had to guess?

"I'm on shift, anyway. Can't be fighting in here," Mason said, as if he had to offer up some reason for not getting into a fight right then.

Boys are so weird...

"Let's go, Clara," Caleb said as he walked around Mason and Silas and started pulling me towards Laruen and Emmy.

"Hey, you should join us, Mason. When's your break? We've got somewhere to go nearby," Ralph asked. I saw Mason look towards the kitchen as if he needed to consider it before giving an answer.

We got seated quickly, and at Laurens request, Mason wasn't the one in charge of our table. "I'm telling you that he didn't do it on purpose," Emmy kept repeating. "I didn't like how he was looking down at you," Lauren said resolutely.

"Wait until she hears I invited him to come with us after," Ralph whispered just a bit too loud to Caleb. "You did what?!" Lauren shrieked.

"That's right, we never explained why we're even here," Caleb told Silas as he was suppressing his laughter. "It's a tradition Ralph and I started a few years back. At the start of every baseball season in the Spring, we come up to the tallest mountain in the state and go to a spot him and I discovered when we were kids."

Silas looked over to Lauren, Emmy, and I with an upraised eyebrow. "You guys don't know what this spot is, do you?"

"Clara and I have just been dating for nine months; we weren't together this time last year," Caleb answered immediately. I had just started to shake my head no, but Caleb's answer almost caused me to choke.

It was obvious that Caleb wanted to make a point of how long we had been dating.

"Makes sense," is all Silas answered, his eyes stuck on the empty plate in front of him. His smile was crooked, with one end slightly raised higher than the other. It was an altogether humorless smile and seeing it put my stomach in knots.

"Silas, um…" Emmy tucked her hair behind her ear, clearly trying to gather her courage. "I'm glad you came along."

I sat up straighter on my chair, surprised. Who'd have thought Emmy could be so direct like this. The comment hadn't been directed at me and yet I feel like I was the one that was flirted with.

Silas narrowed his eyes slightly at Emmy, a coy smile on his face. "Glad to be here," he answered.

"Yeah, god knows we need more guys to counterbalance the goofballs we girls have to deal with here," Lauren said with a scoff.

Caleb leaned back on his chair, pretending to be offended. "Hey, I'm no goofball. Ralph on the other hand…"

Ralph got up and punched Silas in the arm playfully to retaliate.

Everyone ordered their food and started eating. I

noticed Mason kept shooting Lauren looks while he was waiting tables around us, several of which Lauren happened to return. Whenever their eyes met, Lauren would hurriedly look away with a pout.

No matter how hard I tried, I couldn't get over the pain I felt in my chest as I thought of Silas's reaction to what Caleb had said. Eventually, the pain became too much for me to bear.

"Sorry guys, gotta use the bathroom," I blurted out as I hastily got to my feet. I washed my face in the bathroom with what had to be the coldest water known to man. I stared at my reflection and tried to control my breathing.

What's gotten into me? I asked my reflection. *What is this pain I feel in my heart?*

I shook my head and tried to get my thoughts in order. Just as I was starting to feel ready to rejoin the others, Lauren walked into the bathroom.

"You ok, Clara?" she asked. "Everyone finished eating. The checks already paid, too." I took a deep breath, trying to relax before answering.

"Seeing him with Emmy is too much, huh?" she asked, ruining my attempt to calm down.

"What are you talking about? This is…" I trailed off.

Lauren gave me a knowing look. She went to the mirror and fixed her hair. "You ever ask yourself if he's hurting like you are when he sees you with Caleb?"

The question caused a pit to form in my stomach. "What if he's suffering in silence? Just a thought."

Could that be…true?

A reflexive hand shot up to my chest. *Could he be feeling this same pain?*

Without another word, she left the bathroom again. I blinked at the door for a few moments before following after her.

"Everyone's outside waiting," Caleb said as I approached the table. It was empty except for him.

Caleb wordlessly extended his hand, inviting me to take it. I reached out and linked my fingers through his, though I felt a bit of apprehension as I did. I stood rooted to the spot, staring at our joined fingers. "You alright?" he asked, concerned. "I—I'm fine," I stuttered.

As we rejoined the others, I realized Ralph was looking over me at someone who was also leaving the restaurant at the same time. "Invitation still open, right?" Mason asked Caleb as he walked beside us. "You know it," Caleb responded.

Lauren made a face when she saw Mason approaching, but she held herself in check. It looked like Emmy had finally gotten to her, as she didn't make a scene or complain.

"Now, shall we start heading to the spot?" Ralph asked when he had the attention of everyone in the group. "Lead the way," Caleb said.

"This way, everyone!" Ralph exclaimed. "Showboat," I whispered at Lauren and Emmy with a smirk. "Dork, more like," Lauren added.

Beside the restaurant was a hiking trail that took you to the top of Mount Raven. Ralph started following the main trail but took a diverging path along the way. The trial was already rugged, but the second path was even worse. I started having to focus even more on my footing.

"Hey, Silas, that's a sick bike you have by the way," Ralph called out from the front of the group. "Oh, you ride a motorcycle?" Mason asked, interested. "I wish I could have one, but I won't be able to have one until I move out."

"You, on a motorcycle? Oh, I'd love to see that," Lauren mocked. "I seriously can't tell if you're being sarcastic or not," Mason deadpanned.

"You've gotta see it," Caleb answered.

"Thanks," is all Silas said in reply. His response and tone were duller than usual. I thought again about what Lauren had told me in the bathroom about him suffering.

I shot him a quick glance, which was hard to do since he was walking behind me. I realized with a start that he and Emmy were walking side by side, having a quiet conversation with each other. Emmy was walking up close to him, her hands filling the space between them.

I closed my eyes and tried to focus on anything else that wasn't them, and yet I couldn't help but feel happy that Silas's hands were buried deep in his pockets.

It turned out that looking behind made me more distracted than I thought, because I made a bad step and started to slip. I braced myself. There were rocks beneath us, and I was headed straight for them. Thankfully, I feel strong arms reach out and catch me before I hit the ground.

Considering Caleb was standing right beside me when I started to slip, I opened my eyes and started thanking Caleb for saving me. And yet, when I opened my eyes, it was *Silas* who was holding me tightly in his arms.

"Uh—I—" I blinked several times in succession, trying to process my thoughts. This was way more physical contact than we had ever had, and the feeling of having his arms around me caused my heart to quicken. His eyes were calm, yet his body hot. He had been quite a few paces back, and I had no idea how quickly he had to move to catch me.

Yet there I was, safe in his arms.

"Wow, Silas, nice catch!" Ralph called out. "Hey, are you alright?" Lauren moved by Mason to ask.

Silas's grasp of me lasts for just a moment longer than necessary. His grip tightened around me, and my eyes jumped from his left and right eyes repeatedly. The moment he released me; all sorts of thoughts flooded my mind. Most notable of all was the selfish thought of wanting the moment to last longer.

"Thanks, Silas," I finally managed to say. Silas took a deep breath, as if he's relieved.

"Watch your step," he answered sternly.

Even though the moment's passed, my cheeks continue to burn. Our faces had never been that close together, and I can't help but replay the moment over in my head over and over.

I looked over at Caleb absentmindedly, but the look he was giving me shook to my core. There was no doubt about it; he caught the way I was looking at Silas.

I opened my mouth to explain, but Caleb's eyes shot up to the cap on Silas's head.

"I recognize that logo," Caleb said under his breath. "It's you…isn't it?"

Ralph walked up to Caleb and placed a comforting hand on his shoulder. "What's going on, man?"

"You used to live on Clara's street years ago. You were the guy she used to know, isn't that right, Clara?"

I took a frightened step back. Caleb's voice was low and angry, and he was giving me a furious look.

"Caleb…stop. Please calm down—"

"Calm down? After nine months of dating, the *one thing* you kept from me is that *this* is the guy? The one you used to run off with every day after school?"

"…That's all in the past, Caleb. It doesn't matter anymore," I urged, but my voice lacked any sort of conviction. It was clear that I didn't believe in the words myself.

"It matters now! He's back, and suddenly you're going to his house, inviting him to your job…Don't pretend, Clara. You're *thrilled* he's back. And you," Caleb swung his focus fully onto Silas, moving aggressively into his space. "You think you can just wander back into town and take Clara? That you two could just pick up where you two left off?"

Silas remained steady, his voice calm but dangerous. "She's not a *possession*, Caleb. She's not a trophy you get to claim."

"She was my girlfriend before you decided to play high school hero and involve yourself in things that don't pertain to you. You left, I *stayed*. I'm the one who picked up the pieces when you abandoned her."

Caleb took another step closer to Silas, his voice seething with rage. "Don't think I haven't seen the way you look at her, waiting for a chance to make your move."

Silas took a step forward, closing the distance between them. "You're right. I shouldn't have left. But if she wants to talk to me now, that's her choice. Not yours to control."

"Oh, *trust* me, I've made my choice. And my choice is to end this."

Caleb shoved Silas hard, intending to start the fight. "*No!*" I shouted, trying to get in between them, but Lauren held me back from getting in harm's way.

"Wait—"

"Don't!"

Mason and Lauren yelled at the same time, but it was too late. Silas lunged forward at Caleb and landed a strong blow to his right cheek. Caleb staggered backwards but recovered quickly. He spat some blood on the floor before clenching both of his fists and charging at Silas in a blind rage.

"Hey, stop!" Ralph yelled. I watched in horror as Silas and Caleb were all over each other, exchanging blows. Ralph hooked his arms around Caleb and pulled him back, but it was obvious that Caleb wouldn't be held back for long. Emmy placed both of her hands over her ears, afraid. Once she knew I wouldn't try to intervene anymore, Lauren moved forward and got between the two boys, trying to end the fighting. She tried raising her voice to make everyone stop, but it was no use.

My hands went up to my mouth as I witnessed what happened next. I wasn't sure who threw the punch— it all happened in a blur. But Lauren fell to the ground, her hand on her cheek.

She had just been hit in the face.

"Hey!" Mason roared, so angry he was trembling. He ran up to Silas and pushed him with everything he had. It was obvious that seeing Lauren on the ground had taken all the fight he had in him, because the push sent Silas straight to the ground.

Mason shielded Lauren with his body and pulled her away. "The hell's wrong with all of you," is all he said as he escorted Laruen back to the restaurant. Lauren kept a shaking hand over her cheek as she let Mason guide her wordlessly. Emmy lowered her hands from her ears and looked like she was ready to start crying. She walked after Mason and Lauren without looking back a single time.

Caleb and Ralph were breathing hard; their eyes focused on Silas. I looked over at him still on the ground, expecting to see him fuming. And yet his eyes were solely on me. They looked wounded, as if what Caleb had said had gotten to him.

I'm the one who picked up the pieces when you abandoned her.

"Come on, get up. We're not done," Caleb said as he looked down at Silas on the ground.

Silas broke his eye contact with me and looked up at Caleb. He was starting to get up to his feet, but I pushed past and stood directly in front of Caleb. My hands trembled, fueled not by fear, but by a furious, icy clarity.

"Don't you dare come near him, Caleb. Don't you dare."

"He *attacked* me, Clara! You saw all of it. He's dragging you into—"

"Stop this…I'm warning you, Caleb. *Stop.*"

Caleb started to shake his head slowly from side to side.

"I see how it is," he said with a shaky breath. "We're done, Clara. I've had enough. I'm liberating you. You're free to be with Silas all you want now."

I stared at Caleb in disbelief as he lingered in front of me, looking at me with a pained expression. He shot one final look at Silas behind me before storming off, Ralph walking behind him.

Caleb had taken a few steps before I found my voice again.

"Caleb, wait—"

"Oh, so you *do* have a voice?" he asked condescendingly. "I was beginning to think you'd let me walk away without saying anything at all."

Caleb didn't turn around; he spoke over his shoulder with his voice barely louder than a whisper.

"Goodbye, Clara."

I didn't move for a long time. I continued repeating the moment over in my head, unable to process the sadness I felt.

Eventually, I looked up from the ground only for my breath to catch when I realized Silas had gotten to his feet and was standing in front of me. His gaze was fixed on me, looking like I was the only thing that existed in the entire world.

He gently checked me for injuries, and I insisted I was fine. He had scrapes from the fight, but he was mostly fine, too.

I didn't mean for them to start while Silas was looking right at me, but the tears just started forming on their own. He approached me without a word. He extended one of his hands and he started to softly caress my face. He used his thumb to gently wipe one of my tears as it rolled down my cheek.

Silas and I shared an intense, lingering moment of eye contact. His hand was still on my cheek, and I didn't move it away.

"I'm sorry about Caleb…" he said softly. I didn't answer, I just nodded quietly.

"I didn't abandon you, you know," Silas said under his breath. "I know, Silas," I whispered back.

"Everything back home was chaos, a fight I couldn't win. I'm tired of drifting. I just want this to be the start of something real—a life I chose."

"There's something I've been meaning to tell you, Clara." Silas grabbed one of my arms, as if he couldn't bear me pulling away from him. "You have this strength…this worth. Ever since I heard you became a reporter, I started to read your work. I could see you interwoven into all your words. I've always looked up to you, Clara. And seeing that is what gave me the push I needed to come back…the push to come and see you."

Silas's expression was one of absolute resolution.

He looked directly at my eyes, unwavering. He swallowed, hard, and I widened my eyes, my mind going blank from expectation

"Is… is that true?" I managed to ask. Silas nodded.

"I've always kept tabs on you. And I've read your feature. You're the real deal, *Ms. Reporter.*" Silas's words came out so confident that I couldn't help but believe him.

My eyes drifted down to my feet. "Sometimes I feel like it was just luck… that anyone could have done what I did—"

Silas placed his hands on both of my cheeks and gently directed my attention back to him. I stared into his eyes, transfixed.

"Enough of that," he urged. "You are enough, Clara. You are."

Silas took a deep breath, and I wondered if he was about to kiss me.

"At the very least, you're enough for *me.*"

My breath caught, and I felt like my heart was going to beat straight out of my chest.

Suddenly, I watched as something clouded Silas's eyes. He pulled back. Though I knew I shouldn't feel this way, considering Caleb had just broken up with me, I was filled with immense disappointment as Silas dropped his hands from both sides of my face.

"We should get going," he said somberly as he started to massage the back of his neck. I didn't know the reason behind him pulling away, but I felt thankful for it at the moment. It gave me a chance to calm myself down.

"Mm," Is all I could reply as Silas started walking back down the path we came from.

10

Silas and I rejoined the others near the entrance to Cliff Point. Ralph and Caleb were gone, meaning they took off after the fight. I couldn't help but wince, realizing that things between Silas and the guys couldn't possibly be worse than they are right now.

"Thank you for holding me back," Silas directed at Mason. Mason didn't give much of a reply.

"Can I borrow you for a second?" Silas asked Lauren. She lifted her eyes off the ground for the first time since we approached. She nodded, and they walked off to the side. I could tell from his body language that Silas was apologizing to her, his eyes glued to her slightly swollen cheek.

While I watched Silas and Lauren, my eyes started to drift towards Cliff Point when something caught my eye.

An employee, clearly one that works in the kitchen,

opened a back door carrying a large garbage bag. With one effortless swing, he threw the bag into a large dumpster located behind the restaurant. The man wiped his hands together quickly, though it looked more like a gesture of completion rather than an attempt to get dirt off of his hands. During that gesture, my eyes were drawn to the man's rolled-up sleeves.

"Hey, Mason?" I asked when Silas and Lauren rejoined us. "There's a bald guy that works with you in the restaurant, the big guy with the beard?"

Mason took a moment to stare blankly at me for a moment before answering. "Yeah, I know who you mean. What about him?"

"How long has he been working here? Do you remember around when he started?" Mason walked up to the same wall Lauren was at and started leaning against it just beside her. Lauren didn't so much as flinch, letting her shoulder almost brush up against him.

"I think just about a month ago? It wasn't very long, honestly." I brought up a hand to my chin. "Did anything about him strike you as odd? Maybe his behavior?"

"Is something up?" Lauren asked me, perking up. Her mood was much more uplifted after hearing Silas's apology, but when she heard this, she looked back to her normal self.

"No, I'm just curious about something," I told her.

Lauren's face lit up light a lightbulb, clearly remembering our conversation from before the gondola ride. She leaned in closer to Mason unconsciously, though I noticed Mason didn't move away from her at all.

"So, about the bald guy?" I directed at Mason.

I kept my eyes squared onto him. Mason blinked at me several times before answering. "I was closing one night, and it was just the two of us. I was cleaning the front of the restaurant, and he was cleaning the kitchen. All of a sudden, I heard the breaking of a glass, but it wasn't just the sound a glass makes when it falls on the ground. No, this glass was thrown against the wall."

Mason shifted his body and crossed his arms. "I walked to the back to see what was up only to see him cleaning up the glass with a broom. I asked him about it, and he told me he had these anger issues he was dealing with. He told me he was working hard to get over them. He didn't ask me directly, but I knew he hoped I wouldn't tell anyone else about it. I've seen him do his job and he does it well. That's the only episode I've seen where he's broken anything."

"You never reported it or anything?" Lauren asked. Mason shook his head. "He'd be fired if he did anything like that when the managers are around anyway. Also, I told myself if he kept breaking glasses that I'd speak up. Nothing ever happened again."

Emmy walked up to me and placed one of her hands on my back. If the gesture was for her comfort or for mine, I honestly couldn't tell.

"Did you want to talk to him? Is there anything else you need?" Emmy asked. "Yeah, you want me to take a photo of him?" Lauren chirped. She didn't have her camera with her, but I knew that if I asked, she'd come back with a borrowed camera and do it in a heartbeat.

"No, no, don't worry," I said as I waved both of my hands. As much as I would've loved to set Lauren up for a stakeout photoshoot, today wasn't the day.

"Why ask about him?" Mason asked, his voice curious.

I took a deep breath before answering. "Two investigators came to my house not too long ago. They asked me some questions about my feature."

"Seriously?"

"No way…"

Emmy and Mason said at the same time.

Lauren looked over to Silas and huffed, disappointed. "You *also* knew? I thought I was the only one!"

Silas looked like he wanted to say something, but after shooting a quick look at me, he seemed to decide on saying something else.

"I was a part of the story. The investigators wanted me there, so we got interviewed together. That's all."

I looked over to Lauren. "Can you show everyone the pictures I asked you to bring?" She nodded, pulling out the pictures from her bag. She distributed them to the group, keeping one to herself to show Mason.

"Wait," Mason murmured. "That's the same tattoo as…"

"Right," I cut him off. "Your coworker has the same tattoo as the guys from the farmer's market. They're connected somehow."

Emmy stared at the picture in her hands. "What does this mean, Clara?"

Remembering that it was Silas who asked me for the pictures in the first place, I looked over to see Silas's reaction.

Silas was dissecting the picture, his face strewn with concern. There was no doubt in my mind; Silas *recognized* that tattoo from somewhere. Clearly, though, he wasn't going to say anything about it right now.

"I can ask my coworker about it—"

"No, no, I don't want to bring any more attention to ourselves," I interrupted as I shook my head at Mason. He furrowed his brow at me.

"Clara, you had investigators at your door. I think it's a little too late for that," Mason said.

"What are you suggesting Clara? That all of these men are a part of a gang?" Emmy asked quietly.

"There's more, though. It's not just the men with the tattoos," I said. "Tell them about what we found at the library, Clara," Lauren urged. I nodded at her before continuing.

"Lauren and I met up at the library to comb over old newspaper editions. We found one from over a month ago, an advance copy that covered kidnapping of a girl in town. The paper that was actually got released didn't have that story, so no one got to read about it."

Emmy gasped, and the entire group went silent.

"A…kidnapping?" Emmy spoke slowly. "Wouldn't everyone be talking about it?" she asked.

"The girl was saved, but the kidnapper is still at

large, according to the story," Lauren spoke up.

"That would explain why no one was noticeably missing. The entire thing was covered up, most likely by police. The police might've told the family to keep quiet about the kidnapping while they investigated," I answered.

"What are you saying, then? That there's some sort of conspiracy going on? Something that involves not just the kidnapping but also the men with the tattoos?" Emmy asked.

All of us except Silas, who was still staring at the photo, regarded Emmy silently.

I gathered all of my courage to say what was in my heart. The person whose eyes I decided to lock onto as I said it was Silas's, who chose right that moment to look up from the picture.

"I want to get to the bottom of this, you guys. For a reason that's beyond me, I've stumbled upon this, and I want to learn the truth about what's going on."

Silas fixed me with an unyielding gaze. I held strong, refusing to let my own gaze falter under his resolute stare.

Are you with me, Silas? I asked from deep within my heart.

"Wait," Mason said. He raised a hand into the air questioningly. "You already had two investigators at your doorstep, and you want to dig deeper?"

"What do you suggest we do, just sit back and do nothing?" Lauren asked. Mason gave her a look. "Well, do you want more cops showing up to your house, to all of our houses?"

"I get it, you want answers. I think I'm with you on that," Emmy said.

"I'm just trying to play devil's advocate here," Mason insisted. "I don't think the fact that the kidnapping was covered up is that serious. It's probably still an ongoing investigation, that's all. The cops are already on the case. Even if there was some sort of conspiracy going on, they already showed up to Clara's. They'll get to the bottom of it."

"Sure, then we'll never find out the truth," Emmy said under her breath. Mason looked at her questioningly.

"Things have a way of getting swept under the rug," I spoke up in place of Emmy. "I agree. The best way to confirm that the truth gets out is to get to the bottom of it myself."

"When did the kidnapping happen?" Silas asked suddenly. I gave him a knowing look. "I think you've already figured it out, but the kidnapping is *definitely* the reason behind the curfew in town."

Mason raised his eyebrows but didn't say anything. "That explains it so much better…" Emmy trailed off.

"What's the next move, Clara?" Silas asked. I shot Silas a quick glance. "I'm…not sure."

The group was quiet for a beat. "What do you guys think?" I asked.

"I don't know about all of this, but this tattoo business and the kidnapping caught my attention," Mason answered. "If there's anything I could do to help, just let me know."

"Me too!" "Yes, me too!" both Lauren and Emmy

chirped.

Silas and I locked eyes again, and an affirming look flashed on his face. I smiled at him warmly.

"Thanks, all of you. For listening to me and for offering to help," I told them all sincerely.

We all started to head to the gondola when—

"Wait, Lauren, can I talk to you for a second?" Mason called out. I saw Lauren's shoulders jerk up as she heard his voice. Her eyes jolted at everyone in our group as all our heads turned in her direction. Her cheeks reddened significantly. Without a word, she turned right around and walked right back to Mason.

"They're adorable," Emmy whispered into my ear as she pulled me aside from Silas. I gave her a smile. Lauren couldn't seem to keep her eyes on Mason, meanwhile his eyes didn't seem to want to be anywhere else except on hers.

"I'm happy for Lauren. I kept telling her that Mason wasn't so bad." I nodded at her in agreement. "It's a good thing Ralph left early and missed this, though," Emmy sighed. I stiffened as I thought about him and how heartbroken he'd be when he found out about this development.

"He's liked her for a long time, but she never gave him any signs of being into him at all. It was always one-sided. I hope he gets the hint now so that he can move on," I answered.

Lauren rejoined us not long after, followed by Mason, but she refused to look at any one of us directly. I tilted my head to the side curiously. What could Mason want?

"You guys don't have rides anymore, do you?" Mason mused. Emmy and I shared a look.

"Oh, right…" I said. Silas could take one of us with him, but that left two other girls stranded. Mason started to laugh watching the gears in both of our heads turn.

"My shift ends in another hour. You can all hang out at the restaurant until I wrap up, then I could drive you all home," he offered. He gave Silas a quick look. "Sound good to everyone?"

Silas massaged the back of his neck. "Looks like there's no other choice," he said.

Emmy, Lauren, and I took him up on the offer. I turned to look over at Silas before he left.

"…See you around?" I asked nervously. Silas chortled, giving me a playful look. "Sure, I'll see you."

Just like before, it was right at that moment that I saw a haze settle over his stare. His thoughts seemed distant, and I instinctively took a step closer to him in an attempt to reach him—

But he didn't notice. He turned and headed back to the gondola without another word. I looked at his receding form, somehow expecting that the exchange would involve something *more*, and yet somehow feeling more distant than I did just moments before.

The reason for that distant feeling was something I couldn't figure out.

Lauren started to walk back towards the restaurant entrance alongside Mason, leaving me alone with Emmy.

Emmy walked up to me and gave me a long look.

"So, you knew Silas from years ago," she said suddenly. "He fought hard for you. It was truly a sight to see."

I looked at Emmy, dazed. "What are you trying to say—"

"I've just happened to notice something since I've been keeping a close eye on Silas. It seems to me that among everyone here, the person he's kept constantly in his line of sight has been…you. Even though I was right beside him, you'd monopolize his attention, Clara. And without even trying, might I add. Now that I know that missing piece, the fact that you two have history, everything makes sense."

"Emmy, I—I didn't mean to hide this from you…" I trailed off, worried that I'd hurt her feelings.

"I'm not jealous," Emmy said with a wave of her hand. "Disappointed, sure. It was fun to be with him and like I said he's a gentleman. But from the start I knew he didn't see me in any special way. And after today, I know that the reason he doesn't is because he already thinks of someone else that way."

Having conveyed what she wanted to say, Emmy skipped ahead to catch up to Lauren and hook her arm through hers. She leaned closely and whispered something seemingly teasingly, causing Lauren to jump up in surprise.

She might be shy and timid, but it was obvious that Emmy knew how to keep a close eye on people and notice how they felt. Her directness and ability to say things exactly how they were was something to be admired.

I took a deep breath to try to calm my rapidly

beating heart, the words Emmy had told me on repeat in my mind.

<h1 style="text-align:center">11</h1>

I met Caleb during an after-school volunteering event for a community service club in my junior year. It was before my decision to delve deeper into the world of journalism, so I was still working part-time to help my mom with groceries. Even so, I made time to volunteer when I could.

I was in charge of a welcome table that was placed in the main front entrance of the school. I was given a clipboard with a sign-in sheet and was instructed to request all parents and students to sign their names on the sheet. It was a one-person job honestly, but I was informed that I'd be getting another volunteer to assist me at the table.

I was a few minutes early to the table and had brought a few extra pens of my own to make sure we wouldn't run out in the middle of a huge line. I sat in one of the two empty chairs and waited. Caleb arrived a few minutes late, but I didn't care much once I saw him.

Truth be told, I immediately thought he was cute. I loved his build, the way his shoulders looked in his tight-fitting shirt, and especially the warm smile he gave me when he saw me.

"Nice to meet you. I'm Caleb Rhodes," he said casually as he extended his hand. I blinked at him twice before extending my own. "Hi—I'm Clara Monroe." I wasn't quite used to being offered an outstretched hand, so his formality caught me by surprise.

"This chair's for me, I'm guessing?" he asked as he walked around the table and pulled it back. "Sure is," I answered quietly as I scooted the chair just a hair further away from him in an attempt to give him more space.

"Moving away from me already?" he asked amusingly. "I won't bite, I promise," he said. I looked up at him, feeling embarrassed. "No, I—" I started to say, but suddenly Caleb looked beyond me, his face serious.

Without any sort of hesitation, Caleb pulled the chair from under the table and lifted it off the ground. He walked away from the table, the chair in tow. I looked after him, stunned, to see a few students on the opposite side of the entrance trying to set up some decorations. Caleb placed the chair on the ground in front of them, offering it to them. The students all looked at him happily and started thanking him.

Caleb walked away with a satisfied smile. It wasn't until he walked back to the table that he realized something.

"Uh, you wouldn't happen to have a second chair with you by any chance?" he asked. I shook my head no. "I'll look for another one," he said as he headed into the school.

It took him a few minutes, but he returned with another chair and took a seat just beside me. "I tend to uh, do that," Caleb said embarrassedly.

"Do what?" I asked, curious. "Do things I think are going to help others without realizing what it'll mean for me. Like just now, having to find a chair for myself. Or, signing up for this volunteering event without realizing it conflicts with something else I had planned for later tonight, for example."

The corner of my mouth curled upwards. "So, you do things without thinking them through, basically?" I asked. "You could put it that way," Caleb responded with a reserved laugh.

I couldn't help but admire his steadfast attitude. Caleb makes up his mind to do something almost instantly and goes through with it regardless of the outcome. I felt like I could take a page from that book and could stand to gain a lot if I learned to be more like that.

While he was looking away, I took a moment to check him out from the corner of my eye. "Do you play a sport?" I asked innocently.

"Why do you ask? Because I look like I work out?" he asked flirtatiously. "You have blisters in your hands," I answered. I then turned my head to face him head-on. "But yeah, you do look like you work out. So, there's that."

Caleb looked into my eyes, a smile appearing on his face. "Baseball. I've played it all my life."

Without warning, one of the officers from the community service club in charge of the event approached the table. "Hi you two, we've made a small change to the sign-in sheet…Wait were you two just flirting?" she asked suspiciously.

"Uh, no—"

"No, no we were—"

"Anyway," she interrupted, taken aback. Let me replace the paper in your clipboard…You guys just, keep it up." She then turned back towards the entrance of the school and didn't look back.

"Busted, huh?" Caleb asked. "Someone's confident," I answered, resting my chin on my hand. Truth was, I was nervous. And yet talking this way with him was fun, and I wanted it to continue.

Unfortunately, parents started pouring in and Caleb and I got busy. It was a consistent stream of visitors and the page filled up fast. Without even asking me, Caleb got up and ran into the school to bring us more copies as soon as the page was almost filled up. It felt great to count on him. If I had been alone, I'd have been forced to leave the table alone. For a reason I couldn't explain, it felt like he was happy to be working with me, too.

Parents stopped arriving when the event had officially started, and things quieted down. I was secretly happy for it, since I could talk to Caleb some more. I discretely tried to fix my hair when I saw a car pull up to the front of the school and start honking its horn.

"Come on, Caleb! Let's get going!" a boy called out with the passenger side window down. Caleb looked at the car longingly. I smiled internally, feeling completely helpless against that puppy-dog look of his.

"You should go," I told him earnestly. "The event started anyway. I have extra pages here, too. I should be fine.

"You sure?" he asked me. I nodded in reply. Caleb got right up to his feet and approached me, making me immensely nervous. I closed my eyes reflectively, but all Caleb did was plant a gentle, quick kiss on my forehead.

"Thanks, Clara. And it was nice meeting you," he said as he turned away from the table. "You too," is all I managed to answer.

Caleb only took a few steps away from the table before turning back around. "Can I talk to you tomorrow sometime at school?" he asked.

"I was hoping you would," I answered looking at him defiantly. Caleb smiled back at me in reply, turning back towards the car. I spotted the boy in the car teasing him from the moment he got into the car. I stared after the car as it pulled away from the front of the school.

Caleb and I became a couple just a week after we met during that volunteering event. He was the one that asked to make it official, and I readily agreed. The months went by, and I did feel myself becoming closer to Caleb in that time. And yet, try as I might, I had these walls that I simply couldn't bring down for him. I never opened to him about what had happened with my father, and I never truly opened my heart to him. I also decided to keep certain details about Silas, who was an important part of my past, a secret. I felt that I always kept him at a safe distance, as if I was always wary of him getting too close.

Had I been leading him on this entire time? I can't help but ask myself. It did seem that way, considering how accepting I was to let Silas into my heart and yet made it impossible for Caleb. That hypocrisy alone would be enough to drive anyone to a breaking point; I can see that clearly now.

Caleb saw what I refused to admit: that my love for him was conditional, and my energy was always reserved for the one I truly caved. He broke up with me because of the way I looked at Silas, not just on that day on Mount Raven, but *always*. Caleb realized that he was never going to be enough. And the worst part?

He was absolutely right.

12

"Sweetheart, are you ok?" my mother asked.

After being dropped off at home by Mason, I had stumbled inside. I leaned against the door and slipped towards the floor, my head pressed against my balled-up fists. My mother had pushed open the door only to find me sitting on the other side of it.

It was the violence of the fight and the adrenaline that carried me through up until this point. I held myself together for Silas and my friends, but when I was alone, the dam broke. The truth that my relationship was over begun to settle. It felt like a clean, final cut. Reality was Caleb was gone, I was single, Silas was acting distant, and I was no closer to uncovering the truth about what was happening in Fall River.

I started getting to my feet, wondering just how long I had been in that position for.

"Tell me, what's wrong?" she asked as she walked

into the house and closed the door. When I heard the words, I walked up to her and let her embrace me. I took a deep breath, thankful for the feeling of warmth.

"Did something happen, Clara?" she asked, concern woven into her words.

"We're done, mom. Caleb and I broke up," I sniffed into her shoulder. I could have said *Caleb broke up with me*, but I knew that it was from my own doing. I had already accepted it. Saying that Caleb and I had simply *broken up* felt more appropriate. She was hugging me so tightly I could barely breathe, and yet I didn't care. I willed her to go even tighter. "Oh, honey," she whispered softly.

Knowing how much I loved it, my mother gently ran her fingers through my hair. I started to relax for the first time, and I felt like I could fall asleep right then.

"Did you see forever while you were with him, sweetie?" she asked after a while. The thought that we'd break up never crossed my mind, and yet the thought we'd be together forever didn't either. I never pictured myself in a wedding dress, standing beside Caleb in a tuxedo.

There's no doubt about it: The thought never even crossed my mind with Caleb. Not even in passing.

That's the very reason for the breakup, I wanted to answer.

"No, I didn't," I answered. My mom didn't say anything else; she just continued to stroke my hair as I cried softly onto her shoulder, the tears fueled by a mix of guilt and loss. My heart was a jumbled mess, struggling to get move past the pain of the breakup and the terrible realization that Caleb had been right all along.

***

In what I suspected to be an attempt to clear up my mind, my mother sent me on a quick grocery run even though we could go another few days without it. I walked to the store with my eyes almost exclusively on the ground, raising it only when I had to as I meandered through the grocery aisles.

I sniffed, feeling the urge to cry rising again in my throat. I lifted my sleeve over my wrist and brought it up to my eye to wipe the tears that were welling up in my eyes when I suddenly bumped into someone.

"Sorry," the stranger said.

"That's my fault—" I started to respond but froze when I looked up and realized the person I'd just bumped into was Silas.

He had a faraway look in his eyes, and to my astonishment, he hadn't realized that I was standing right in front of him. He continued walking as if I were nothing more than a stranger.

A part of me wanted him to continue walking so that he didn't see the bags under my eyes and the puffiness of my nose. But that feeling was overshadowed by the desolation I felt at the thought of Silas treating me like a nobody. It felt like a knife was being slowly pushed into my chest over my heart, an excruciating pain that grew progressively worse.

I extended a nervous hand and started to open my mouth when Silas suddenly stopped walking. He stood, motionless, for a long beat. As if he had suddenly made up his mind about something, Silas suddenly turned right around and nearly walked right into me for a second time.

His face was inches away from my own before he blinked to attention, seeing me for the first time.

His eyes widened into saucers as he saw me, as if I were a magician who had just performed an appearing act before him.

"…Clara?"

"Er—um, hi, Silas," I spoke nervously. I wasn't expecting to run into him so soon after the last time we saw each other. The entire thing caught me off guard, causing me to look down at my feet nervously. I was waiting for him to ask me about my puffy eyes and nose, and to ask if I was ok.

"Hey, Clara," Silas said, sounding grave. I looked up at him, yet he was massaging his neck while looking to his left at nothing in particular. "We have to get to the bottom of this conspiracy, right? No matter what?"

I stared at him blankly. I fought with everything I had against the disappointment I felt from Silas not realizing I had just been crying. He was always so attentive to things like that…

"R—right," I answered, somewhat subdued.

After everything that happened at Mount Raven, I started to feel that the invisible enemy I was fighting felt utterly hopeless. I didn't have a clear first step to take, and the evidence I had felt like it amounted to nothing. The mystery felt like a ghost story, impossible to prove, impossible to pin down.

Continuing to try to uncover the conspiracy felt like picking up a shovel against an entire city of secrets, and now that I was without Caleb, I felt like I was standing alone, with no map and no idea where to even start digging.

Now, something else was taking up most of my attention, and that something was Silas. I played with my sleeves shyly, holding on to hope that he'd still come around and notice something was off with me.

I flinched when I noticed Silas starting to clench his fists in anger. "What if the truth isn't something you want to hear..." Silas trailed off.

Silas had officially lost me. I looked up at him, utterly confused. Silas shook his head, trying to clear whatever mess he had in his head.

"Listen, Clara. I'm going to leave town. There's something I need to find out for myself."

What...?

For a second, I didn't breathe. I didn't blink. I just stared at Silas, feeling empty inside.

This can't be happening...

"Please understand. See you, Clara," he said me as he walked away, distracted.

Please don't go...

I watched him walk away, feeling like he was leaving me behind once again. It was that day those four years ago all over again, and I'd never felt more hollow.

***

I reached under my bed and fished out the shoebox from under it. I looked at the rainbow and pink star stickers on the top and tried to remember what exactly was inside of it. I remembered that the box was related to Silas, but nothing more.

Having steeled myself, I quickly reached out and removed the lid like trying to rip out a band aid. It's a good thing I did, too, because no amount of mental preparation could have prepared me for what was inside.

The largest object in the box was a plastic flower. It was a flower Silas had bought me after I had told him that my favorite color was yellow. He surprised me with it on my birthday; a moment I was confident I'd never forget. The sight of him shyly offering the flower to me made me sigh.

Beside the flower were a series of letters. There weren't many, just a handful. My eyes started to tear up again, and I repositioned myself on the floor so that I could lean against my bed. The letters were from the week that I was sick, and Silas's mother prevented him from seeing me. It would've been too troublesome to talk on the phone, since I'd have to be in the living room so that I could use the house landline phone. We couldn't see each other physically, so we agreed to write each other letters. He'd walk up to my front door to pick up my letter to him, and he'd leave his response letter to the last one I'd written.

I blinked multiple times in succession, trying to get my tears to stop blurring my vision.

Now that I thought of it, that was the first time I

realized I liked writing so much. Was Silas directly responsible for my interest in journalism in the first place?

Picking up the letters, I filtered through them and read the dates. I was only sick for a week, and we stopped writing them after we saw each other again. A part of me wished we had kept that going, especially after he moved so far away.

As I continued to look through the box, the small items instantly brought back sentimental memories, all linked to Silas. At the very bottom of the box was a photo of the two of us, our arms around each other playfully. One of my tears falls directly onto the photo, just beneath our smiling faces.

"Clara, honey," my mom called out as she knocked on the door. I made no effort to wipe my tears or hide the box. I wasn't going to hide from this; not anymore. "Yes, mom?" I answered. She didn't open the door, opting to continue talking to me from the other side of it.

"It's about Silas…" she trailed off.

"Mom, what's going on?" I demanded; all sorts of alarm bells going off on my mind.

"I was at his Lisette's, when Silas just came home. He wouldn't say why but he just said that he's leaving…that he's going to be leaving town. He picked up the house phone and spoke to someone over the phone—"

I pulled my door open so hard it slammed against the opposite wall. I ran out into the hall and straight to our front door.

This won't be like last time, at the supermarket…

"Good luck, sweetie!" she called out as I almost ripped the front door from its hinges, pulling all my weight on it. I'm thankful that I never took off my shoes, because I hit the sidewalk and started running with everything I have.

This time, I'll take action. I'll stop him…!

I focused on Silas's house and saw him backing out from his driveway on his bike. His body was turned away from me, so he didn't see me coming up from the sidewalk.

My feelings…

If he drove off in the opposite direction, I knew I'd never reach him. But if there was any chance that he headed my way…

Please…

Silas continued to back up and jolted forward. It seemed that my prayers had been answered, because he was quickly approaching. Once I saw him coming in my direction, I ran out into the middle of the street and extended my arms out in both directions, my eyes focused solely on Silas's approaching form.

Reach him!

Should he have chosen to drive right past me, there was nothing I could have really done to stop him. And yet, he slowed his motorcycle down and stopped just a few feet in front of me, the front wheel pointed right at me. He placed a foot on the ground and removed his helmet to face me eye-to-eye.

"Don't—go!" I sputtered, putting every fiber of emotion I could muster into the words.

"Clara—"

"Stay, Silas!" I interrupted. I closed my eyes and bent over at the waist, screaming almost at the top of my lungs towards the ground:

"Where are you going, Silas? You look like you're leaving for good this time…stay here—stay with me, Silas."

I gathered all my courage to look up at him. He was facing off to the right, clearly doing his best to avoid my gaze.

"I told you, Clara. I'm not coming back until I have answers. The people behind this, whoever they are, have power. Real power. I need to get to the bottom of this for us."

"*Us?* You say you're doing this for us, but you're not telling me anything, are you? You're making all the decisions, and you're walking away again. This is exactly what happened four years ago, when you pushed me away instead of talking to me before you moved away."

Silas turned to face me, his gaze intense. "This isn't about four years ago. You don't see the scale of what's happening. This involves destroying the lives of people in this town. I can't stop for anything until I find that proof…can't you see that?"

I stepped closer to him, my voice tight as I suppressed the pain I felt as best I could. "All I see is the same thing, Silas. I see you turning your back and leaving Fall River…leaving me…because the problems got too messy. I just lost Caleb because I wasn't brave enough to trust him with the truth of our shared past.

Now, I look at you, and I see you walking away to deal with your world, and it just proves I don't deserve the fight, either. I thought, maybe this time, you were fighting for *us*. But you're just running away, aren't you?"

Silas looked down towards the ground, his shoulders slumping forward slightly. "Four years ago, leaving you without saying goodbye was a mistake," he said.

The change in topic caught me off guard. I felt the tears forming in my ears start to brim over.

"And I never stopped thinking about you even for a day, you know."

"Why did you come back if you're so willing to leave me behind again without explaining why, Silas?" I breathed, my voice cracking. "Please, tell me *why*."

"This isn't about me being *willing* to leave you. If I tell you everything, if I let you come with me, you become the target. I have to leave you out of this, and I have to go alone, because I can't risk you."

I took another step towards him, dropping my voice to a fierce, raw whisper. "You don't get to decide my risk, Silas. Don't you *dare*. If you leave me here in the dark, I will find another way in. I'll go to the police; I'll go to the press. I'll tell anyone who'll listen, even though I don't have sufficient evidence. I will burn this whole thing down myself if that's the only way to prove you can't just abandon me and leave things like this."

Silas's resolve shattered in front of my eyes. He cursed under his breath, his hand coming up to massage the back of his neck. He realized what I was implying; I was threatening to self-sabotage. If his goal was avoiding making me a target, then the worst thing I could do was start sounding alarms. Even without sufficient evidence, going to the police or the press would place an immense target on my back.

"Damn it, Clara. You're impossible," Silas said with a harsh, ragged sigh. He tilted his head towards the ground for a second before looking up and meeting my eyes.

"You're right. I'm sorry. This is the last thing I wanted to make you feel. Especially after what happened four years ago…"

Tears began to fall down my eyes freely now. Once he saw my tears, Silas quickly got off his bike and set down the kickstand. He walked right up to me and pulled me into him, making me feel like the ground beneath my feet had disappeared as I felt Silas against me. I sobbed quietly into his shoulder, my hands hanging limp at my sides.

"Hey, Clara. I'm not abandoning you," he urged. "Not now…not ever."

I reached out and wrapped my arms around him, pulling him somehow closer, making sparks go off in my mind.

"Listen, I need to go alone for this part. But I won't leave you guessing. From this moment on, you get the truth first. Every piece. We're in this together. I promise. Just know that I'm not running away."

Silas pulled away slightly, giving me enough space to look up and meet his piercing gaze. "Unlike four years ago, I'm doing this so there's something left to come back to."

"Write me, then," I insisted. "If you want to prove this is different than before, that is."

Silas tilted his head to the side. "Like that week when you were sick?" I felt a pang in my heart knowing he remembered that week. I nodded at him with a sincere smile.

"Deal," he said.

He looked at me for one final, intense moment, sealing the promise. Then, before I could say another word, Silas threw his leg over the motorcycle, and he was gone.

13

Thump! The sound of the stack of papers made as they were dropped onto my desk.

"Clara, this is what you're going to edit for the next issue. Let me know when it's completed. Thanks!"

I leaned back on my chair wistfully. "No worries," I responded.

For a reason I couldn't wrap my head around, after my debut feature story, I had been exclusively assigned editing work. My feature was well received, and many of the reporters that work in my office commended me for my work. And yet, I never got an opportunity to report ever again. In fact, I was never given the chance to even get quotes from anyone, either.

I looked up to the ceiling, knowing perfectly well what that meant. If I was prevented from ever getting field experience, that meant my name would never be recognized. I wouldn't grow as a reporter, and my work as a journalist would have to stick exclusively to editing. Even though there was nothing wrong with editors, I wanted to lean more into on-the-ground reporting to stay side-by-side with Lauren and other photographers, and directly influence the content being produced.

That feature gave me a taste for what it was like to truly create and report on something myself, a feeling that I just couldn't let go of.

I tried multiple times to ask my boss about it, but I got turned down on every turn.

"Your editing work is what we need right now," he'd say. Other times, he'd say that we had too many reporters on the field right now.

What worried me most of all was the fact that my boss seemed less happy to have me in the office. What I originally believed to be a surefire full-time offer once I graduated high school now seemed like a pipe dream.

"Clara," a voice caught me by surprise, jolting my shoulders up as I tensed up. "Hey," Audrey paused, giving me a pitying smile.

"Audrey, hi," I answered, honestly surprised she was even talking to me. As if ordered by the boss himself, all of the community reporters have stopped associating with me. They've stopped offering to teach me things and have taken to just dumping more and more editing work on me, as if cementing that that's where I belonged.

Audrey slid a business card across my desk to me. I picked it up and read the address on the front. "Couple of months ago, I opened up my own column. The address on that card is the address of my office. It's small, but it works. It's not too far from here. Thing is, I haven't been able to find any stories worth publishing. That's the reason why I work as a reporter here."

"Clara," she emphasized, her tone getting serious. "If you ever find anything that needs publishing, and you feel like you can't count on this paper to follow through with it, consider coming here instead," Audrey instructed as she tapped the top of the card with her index finger.

She tilted her head to the side, offering an encouraging smile. "Good luck, Clara," she said before turning her attention back to the work on her desk.

I walked out of the office at the end of my shift depressed and deep in thought, feeling the business card Audrey gave me in my pocket. I saw an empty tree and imagined Silas was leaning against it, waiting for me after work.

Hey, Ms. Reporter, Silas's first letter started off. *Talk to me about work. How are they treating you after that feature of yours?*

Not good, I had said in my letter back to him. Since he wrote first, I had his return address, meaning I could write back.

They aren't giving you a shot to prove yourself, are they?

I took a deep breath as I looked at the tree longingly.

It means the world to me that you think there's any part of me that's worth proving, I wrote back.

Trust me, the only thing you need to be able to tell that much is a working pair of eyes.

I ignored the feeling of knotting in my stomach and started walking towards the nearest bus stop

It's been two weeks since my breakup with Caleb, and a lot of things have changed. Our lunch group now consisted of just Emmy, Lauren and I. Caleb and Ralph started sitting with some other baseball guys. Caleb didn't reach out to me after the breakup. I caught his eyes lingering on me sometimes during lunch and during the rare moments we ran into each other in the halls, but other than that we didn't talk.

I did feel like a piece of me was missing after Caleb ended things. He was a dependable and strong person that I knew I could count on. But I knew that this breakup was for the best. I couldn't keep hurting him, making him believe he could have the entirety of my heart. That would be wrong, and it had to come to an end.

And yet, his absence was nothing compared to the emptiness that I felt now that Silas had left town again. It was obvious, and I knew that it was pointless to deny it. I missed Silas so much that it hurt, and I yearned for him what seemed like every minute of the day.

I boarded the next bus home. During the ride, something caught my attention, and I leaned into the window to stare. I could see the independent publishing company belonging to Audrey. I made a mental note of its small size. For a reason I couldn't explain, I felt like I belonged there. Audreys' advice to go there in case I had a story repeated itself in my mind as I dedicated its exact location to memory. Just in case I lost the business card, I pulled out my spiral notebook to make a note of the address inside of it.

After copying the address and putting away the notebook, something in my bag caught my eye. I pulled out the letters I had stashed in my bag and looked over them with downcast eyes.

Silas kept his word and wrote to me. I got his first letter two days after he left. By now, I had quite the collection of letters from him. I worked out that it took two days for the letters we wrote to reach the other. I had read all of his letters enough times to know them by memory. In handwriting that was unmistakably his, Silas would talk to me about seemingly pointless things like what he ate that day and how he felt about certain things. They may have seemed pointless to anyone else, but I cherished each and new thing I learned about him.

I remembered his latest letter, where he told me that he needed a few more days before he could come back. My eyes glazed over at the last line he wrote before closing out his latest letter:

I miss you, Clara. More than I ever knew was possible. Do you feel the same way, I wonder?

Obviously, I had written back to him.

I pulled the letters to my chest and breathed shakily. Two weeks had gone by since Silas left town, and it felt like my entire life had hit pause. I waited and waited, counting the days until I saw Silas's motorcycle in front of his house again.

Is this what it was like when he left last time? I asked myself. Did I have this feeling of longing that felt so overpowering that I could just choke on it?

I looked outside of the bus window and remembered a conversation I had with my mom yesterday.

"What does it mean to be in love, mom?" I had asked her while we were doing our weekly cleaning. My mom shot me a curious look before answering. "Love is felt differently be everyone, but I think that one thing that is irrefutable is that love is when you can't imagine your life without that person. Love isn't about romantic feelings alone, you know. I love you, for example. I love Lisette, too."

I looked at her, deep in thought. "But I mean to be *in* love. Not just, love." She smiled at the ground, as if she knew I'd clarify the question that way. "Being in love goes beyond just liking someone or being physically attracted to them, sweetheart. I feel like the best way to explain this is by calling it a 'Best Friend Feeling'."

I blinked at her, my body going rigid. I wanted to hear more, and she caught on to that. "The person you're in love with is often the one you feel most comfortable being your whole, true self around. You trust them deeply and feel safe with them, flaws and all."

"Were you in love with dad, mom?"

"I was at one time," she answered melancholically. "But that comfort disappeared after a time. He didn't feel like my best friend anymore, and I never felt truly safe with him."

My mom tilted her side analytically. "Could you say you were in love with Caleb, honey?"

"I guess not," I answered softly, knowing the answer was right after consulting my heart's true feelings.

I gave my mom a curious look. "Did you not like Caleb, mom? You would wince when I'd talk about Caleb sometimes or you'd groan when I'd go out to see him." She sighed deeply, pausing mid-sweep with a broom in her hands. "It's not that I didn't like him, honey. I just didn't think you two were just right for each other, is all."

She placed her elbow on the broom and leaned against it. "As a mother, you want to your daughter to do the right thing and make the right choices. But I wasn't going to impose myself on your relationships. If it was meant to be, then it was meant to be."

I was looking at the floor pensively when I heard her suddenly stifle a chuckle. "You and Silas really were close those four years ago…" she trailed off. "What does that have to do with anything?" I asked, my cheeks burning at the sudden mention of Silas.

But she wouldn't elaborate further than that. I focused my eyes on my reflection on the window. Truth was, I knew exactly what she was talking and insinuating about.

It was obvious to me now that I thought about it.

All of those years ago, Silas truly was my best friend. There was no one else that I felt I could truly be myself around. That 'Best Friend Feeling', was that what I felt with Silas? And if so, why did I convince myself it was just a friendship after all this time?

The answer to that is clear, I knew. It was a defense

mechanism to stop the pain I felt deep in my heart at his absence.

The bus dropped me off at home, and I had to run from the bus stop to my house due to the rain. I used my work bag to protect my hair from the rain and tried to keep the number of puddles I stepped on to a minimum.

Once inside my house, I called out to my mom only to hear nothing back. I smiled, knowing immediately where she'd gone. Ever since Silas first came back, she had started making frequent visits to see Lisette. Ever since I broke up with Caleb, though, it seemed like they had become best friends. Whenever she wasn't home or at work, chances are she was at Lisette's house. The other half of the time, Lisette was over at our house.

I changed out of my work clothes and got into something more comfortable. I was in the middle of drying my hair when I heard a knock on my front door. I walked over to it and looked through the peephole—

What?

I turned the handle of the front door and opened it apprehensively. An officer stood on the other side of it, an officer I recognized as one of the same two detectives that had asked me those questions from before.

"Clara, I'm glad you're home," the officer said solemnly. I picked up on his grim tone and started to feel panicked.

"What's going on?"

"It's your mother, Clara," the investigator said. "The bakery your mother works in was the latest in a string of armed robberies. She's currently admitted to the hospital, recovering from the injuries she sustained during the attack."

***

I sat in the hospital lobby, hunched over with my forehead pressed against my knuckles. My mind was hazy; a mess of thoughts that refused to organize themselves.

Your mother cooperated with the thieves' demands, the officers told me. They had watched the security footage of the incident and were explaining how the incident went down.

It seems that they demanded that your mother move faster in handing them the cash from the register…That is when the attack happened.

I gritted my teeth. Attacking a store employee because they weren't *cooperating* fast enough…

What monster would do this?

My mother was attacked on the side of the head, knocking her out cold. She was currently intubated, but the doctors were thankfully confident that she would make a full recovery.

"You said this was the latest in a string of robberies…" I had asked the detective in the car ride towards the hospital. "I work for the paper. There haven't been any stories or reports of these robberies. So…how is that possible?"

The detective looked at me in the backseat from the rearview mirror. "These robberies…they've all happened *today*, Clara."

That…can't be.

I drowned out the sounds of the hospital lobby. There was an irrefutable truth that I faced, a truth that no matter how hard I tried, I couldn't overlook any longer.

"…Clara!"

I recognized the voice belonging to Caleb, yet I barely reacted to it. He sat next to me and placed a hand on my shoulder.

"I heard about your mom," he said, concerned. "Clara, is she alright?"

I took a deep breath, trying to calm my breathing. His presence was comforting, but the anger I felt about the situation eclipsed any other emotion in my heart at the moment.

"She's going to make a full recovery," I told him. "She's intubated right now."

"Oh, that's great news," Caleb sighed, sounding relieved. "Everyone else is coming, looks like I'm the first one."

I nodded, my body still in the same position as when he arrived. My eyes refused to leave the single spot on the ground that I was staring a hole onto.

"…Clara, the others told me about what you said at Cliff Point, about the conspiracy in town."

I dug my fingers into my hands so tight that my fingers went white.

"Before this, I would've told you that you were onto nothing, but have you heard, Clara? The robberies today were performed by an entire group; they were all working together. They stole I don't even know how much money, and hurt countless people, your mom included. If the police truly were trying to cover crimes up…"

Caleb's voice turned raw and cold. "…Then they can't do that, not anymore. People are getting hurt, Clara. The entire town knows that now."

"It doesn't matter what you would've told me, Caleb. This isn't me chasing an investigation or general curiosity anymore…" I spat. I raised my head from my knuckles for the first time, feeling more determined than ever.

I thought of my mother's terrified face as thieves stormed her job and forced her to hand over cash. I thought of how she moved as fast as she could, and how she was hurt for not doing it to their preference. Those thoughts alone made my last shred of sanity dissolve.

"They hurt my mother. Now, this is *personal.* Nothing will stop me until I take the truth back. *Nothing.*"

14

I let my eyes wander from my ceiling towards my clock on my nightstand.

Finally, I thought. I got up and gathered my things.

Just as I was about to leave the room, my eyes froze on my copy of the local paper, turned open to the page that had my feature. I sighed, a deep sense of anger creeping over me again. I reached out and grabbed it, folding it under my arm.

I did my best to ignore the stillness and eerily quiet house and left in a hurry.

Back on the sidewalk again, I raised my eyes up from the paper. Silas's latest letter said that he'd be arriving around this time. Despite the unease in my heart, I still felt elated when I saw that Silas had kept his word and was back when he said he would be. As I continued to look, though, I saw something that made me freeze in place.

There it was, just like I had imagined and dreamed it all this time. Silas's motorcycle was parked in his driveway. And there he was, standing right next to it with his helmet on. I could tell it was him through the helmet; Silas could have been in a one-piece suit, and I could still recognize that boy.

Yet Silas wasn't alone. Someone had clearly been riding with him. Silas removed their helmet first before taking off his own. As he lifted the person's helmet, a beautiful lock of golden blond hair fell to her shoulders. The girl looked up at Silas and was talking to him while he removed his own helmet.

I blinked at the sight multiple times, wondering if I was in a nightmare. My dreams consisted of me running into his arms, not him having brought a gorgeous blond stranger with him.

I bent over to pick up my paper from the ground and wipe off any dirt it picked up. I tried my best to take a calming breath.

There's a reasonable explanation for this, I thought to myself anxiously. There had to be. I ignored the knots I felt in my stomach and started to approach Silas's house.

As I got closer, I could see Silas talking to the girl amiably, completely relaxed. He looked comfortable with her, more so than he had looked with Emmy while they talked alone. I could feel the individual cracks forming in my heart as little by little it began to break.

A reason…there's a reason…

"Clara!" Silas called out to me. He turned around to

face me, and I expected to see a face of guilt or a look of having been caught red-handed. And yet, he—

Silas walked right up to me and pulled me into a gentle embrace. There was no hesitation in his actions, and the relief and happiness at the sight of me was unmistakable. My arms went slack at the sudden hug, and I dropped the newspaper in my hand. I took a calming breath and pulled Silas closer to me.

I missed you, I told him with my body. *I missed you so much it hurt.*

I wondered if he got the message, but the way Silas raised one of his hands up to the back of my head gently told me he got the message more than clearly.

"I'm so sorry about your mom, Clara…" Silas whispered. "I'm so, so sorry…"

I choked on a sob. "She passed her breathing trials. She's going to be discharged soon," I soothed.

The girl that Silas had brought coughed suddenly, and I pulled away from Silas, embarrassed.

"I think this is yours," the girl said as she offered my paper that fell to the floor. "Oh—right, thanks," I said as I accepted the paper back.

She moved her head a bit closer to me and extended a quick hand to my face. She used a soft finger to wipe a tear that was falling from my cheek that I didn't know was there. I touched my cheek and could feel that they were wet with tears. Embarrassed, I started wiping my face with the sleeves of my jacket.

Silas pretended not to notice me freaking out about my tears and spoke normally. "Clara, this is my stepsister, Dana. She wanted to check out Fall River."

Dana's eyes were unemotive and calculating, but what was breathtaking about her was her beauty. I immediately felt self-conscious as she stared at me, feeling as if she was judging me quietly.

But, most of all, I felt immense relief.

Stepsiblings…I repeated in my head as I sighed deeply in relief. Dana looked at me analytically, a knowing smile creeping onto her face. I started to wonder if she saw through me and could tell what I was thinking.

"Nice to meet you, Clara," she said. "I've heard a lot about you."

"Hey, I wouldn't say—" Silas started to say.

"I could tell from your reaction that Silas never mentioned me. But that's ok, I know he doesn't tend to talk about himself much."

I look beyond her and stare at Silas, confused. She's right that Silas never mentioned her and is right to point that out. What reason would he have to hide her, someone who's been a part of his life when he was away? I brought up Caleb at the first opportunity, and he was my boyfriend. I don't see what the problem is talking about your stepsibling. Especially considering we've been writing to each other frequently while he was away. So many missed opportunities…

"Should we head in?" Dana asked Silas. He nodded at her, and we all walked inside. I noticed a look of apprehension on Silas's face. His eyes looked glazed over as he stared at the bag that Dana had over her shoulder.

"Mom, this is my stepsister, Dana" Silas said

awkwardly. I could tell from her reaction that she wasn't exactly clued into Dana's existence, either.

"Stepsister?!" she asked.

"Geez, you'd think I were evil with how he never told anyone about me…" Dana said under her breath and glared at Silas.

"Dear, you don't know the half of it. That boy wouldn't tell me if a flying saucer came down and abducted the car driving right next to him," Lisette said as she hugged Dana. Dana gave a half-suppressed laugh as she raised her arms to return the embrace.

"It's nice to meet you, honey. I'm happy you're here," Lisette breathed. "I'm happy that I'm here, too," Dana almost whispered.

***

"Did you have to bring an album filled with all the embarrassing stuff, Dana?"

"I wouldn't be fulfilling my duty as your sister if I didn't."

Dana had pulled out a photo album as a gift for Lisette. It was filled with numerous photos throughout the four years Silas was gone. According to Dana, Silas's father remarried fairly quickly after he moved away, so Dana has known him for almost the entirety of his time away.

"Silas only sent me a handful, and they were always so carefully handpicked so I couldn't embarrass him by showing them off," Lisette said. "These, on the other hand, are perfect."

"Mom, please don't get any ideas—"

"Look at him on this one. He looks so cute riding a bike, right?" Dana pointed out. "I remember that day. I fell off my bike and ate asphalt on that hill…" Silas trailed off.

"You seriously like them, Lisette?" Dana asked. "Oh, I love them honey," she answered sweetly.

I got up to my feet and walked to the opposite couch from the others. I grabbed the paper I had brought with me that I had left on the coffee table and started reading the feature over again. My eyes wandered to the very top of the page, where I caught Dana looking at me pensively. Dana suddenly excused herself from Lissette and made her way over to me, her bag in her hands. Silas followed behind her, and the two of them joined me on the couch.

"I'll be right back, I'm taking this to my room," Lissette said as she left the living room.

"Clara, I asked Silas to bring me back with him so that I could meet his mom and deliver that photo album, but I also came to deliver something to you, too."

I swallowed, nervous about what that something could be. It wasn't helping that Dana wasn't very expressive, her face was almost exclusively resting in a neutral expression. I couldn't tell if she was about to pull out something as innocuous as a stack of quarters or something as threatening as a stick of dynamite from her bag. Regardless of what it was, I'm sure she'd still have that unchanging expression.

"I read your feature in the local paper," she

announced. My eyes widened in surprise. "You did?"

"Silas was a part of your feature, and the news reached our father eventually. I was immediately curious about it and subscribed to your paper to have it delivered to me."

Dana shot Silas another look. "My brother—unsurprisingly—forgot to mention it to me on his own. We had to find out about it from someone else." Silas didn't reply, choosing to raise his hands up guiltily.

I winced internally. The only way to read a paper from a different town or city was to visit a local library, get lucky at a specialized newsstand that sold newspapers from other cities, or to subscribe for a delivered copy. Of all the options, subscribing was the most expensive.

"Something about your feature caught my attention. So, I did some digging and found that this was released by Arden Bay's local paper in their issue that followed closely after yours," Dana said as she pulled out a neatly folded newspaper from her bag.

I blinked at the paper. I knew from the return addresses written on Silas's letters he lived in Arden Bay. That meant that Dana not only subscribed to the Fall River paper, but also had a subscription to the local paper, too.

I grabbed the paper, and Dana helped me flip the pages to find what she wanted to show me. "Read this," she said. My eyes scoured the page.

The Town Local: A Beacon of Progress
CITY HALL CELEBRATES RECORD-
BREAKING STATE FUNDING INCREASE!
Mayor Hails "New Era of Fiscal Responsibility and
Public Safety"
By Evelyn Reed, Staff Reporter

City Hall was abuzz yesterday as the Mayor announced a landmark increase in state appropriations, securing an estimated $12.5 million in additional funding over the next two fiscal years.

"This funding isn't just a number; it's a testament to the hard work of our police force," stated the Mayor at a press conference.

My brow started to furrow in disbelief. Crime rates in large cities like Arden Bay were no joke, and even from a small town like Fall River, you heard of the horrific crimes that occur from time to time. I shook my head and continued reading.

A spokesperson confirmed that the city's correctional facilities reported a 28% decrease in their average inmate count for the last quarter. "The city has clearly found a unique solution to an escalating problem," commented a State Budget Analyst.

I sat back on the couch, squinting in confusion. "What's catching your attention about this?" Silas asked me patiently.

"You don't find it strange that they're reporting a 28% decrease in their inmate count right on time for the city to receive additional funding?" I asked him without taking my eyes off the page. I looked at the name of the reporter who wrote the paper.

Evelyn Reed?

"Clara, it's time for me to come clean about everything," Silas said. I gave Silas an analytical look. He purposefully avoided talking about what he was really doing in Arden Bay in all of his letters. It was about time he was going to open up about what was going on.

"You see, Clara—"

"We think our father is involved in whatever is happening between our two towns," Dana interrupted. Silas gave her a crazed look. "Hey, I was going to explain…"

"You had countless opportunities to say it in your letters. It's too late now, I'm going to explain it," Dana said matter-of-factly.

"Wait, wait…" I said, raising my hands. "What are you talking about? Silas's father?"

"I had my doubts at first, Clara, but it wasn't until I saw those pictures Lauren handed out on Mount Raven. That tattoo…I remember seeing it in my father's office somewhere. I remember it being on a paper, or maybe hung up on his wall—"

"Silas and I snuck into his office to look around but we couldn't find anything like that tattoo again, so he must have cleaned up," Dana added.

"You two are going off of Silas's memory of the tattoo alone?" I asked.

Dana leaned over and pointed her index finger over the name of the paper that published the story from Arden Bay. "The Town Local? Silas and I did some digging. The building that houses that paper is the *same* office where our father works."

"What do you think?" Silas asked. I rolled my head back, my eyes pointing at the ceiling. "This might all be related," I answered. "What if I'm not offered a full-time position, and relegated to a desk job, all because of my feature? Maybe this is the missing piece…"

Suddenly realizing something, I snapped my head at Silas. "Wait, if you suspect your father is involved, then why don't you just ask him?"

Dana and Silas both grew eerily silent. For the first time, I saw something akin to fear flash in Silas's eyes.

"…I could never forgive him if he truly is involved in this, especially after what happened to your mother," Silas said, his voice reserved. "But I want irrefutable proof of his involvement before I start accusing him of anything."

"What he's trying to say is that we're both deathly afraid of him. The direct approach won't work. Besides, he'd just deny it anyway," Dana deadpanned. Silas gave her a look but didn't refute it.

"What about your mother, Dana? Wouldn't she know something?" I asked.

"My mom has her own job apart from my dad. They don't work together, so I doubt she has any involvement."

"But what *is* her job?" I insisted. Silas and Dana gave each other a blank stare.

"You guys don't know…do you?"

"What Dana meant earlier is that she is refusing to believe that her mother is involved, to the point where she is refusing to talk to her about this," Silas said.

"What do you mean?" I said, giving Dana a look.

Dana rolled her eyes at Silas. "My mother can be a lot of things, but she isn't involved in this…she can't be, I refuse to believe it. We have a plan, and we're going to stick to it."

I looked down to the Arden Bay paper in my hands. "Let me guess," I paused to point at the name *Evelyn Reed* before continuing. "Your plan involves speaking to this woman, right?"

Silas nodded. "Our father works in that building. If we went in there and asked where The Town Local was, we'd be stopped by the front desk. So—"

"So, Clara, we were hoping you'd be the one to go into the building and find out where it was for us," Dana cut in.

I sat back on the couch. I knew there would be more intricacies to the plan, and that we were covering the gist of it, but it sounded simple enough. The only thing was…

"You're saying we go to Arden Bay, together?" I asked.

Dana smiled, giving me the answer I needed.

"Think about it for now, Clara," Silas said. But I didn't need time to think. I immediately got to my feet and turned to face them on the couch.

"No need. I might have hesitated about this before, but I lost the luxury of hesitation when my mother got hurt."

I set my unwavering eyes on Silas, who sat up straighter on the couch. "Count me in. Let's do this."

"Your mom…" Dana started to say. I shook my head at her. "She's still intubated for at least a few more days. She won't even know I'm gone."

"Sounds like we're set," Silas said with a determined smile. "Let's leave the day after tomorrow."

***

Lisette had returned to the living room and was in deep conversation with Dana, while I had wandered into the kitchen followed by Silas.

"So that treatment at your job is still going on, huh?" Silas asked. I scoffed. "If I sat on my hands and waited, I'd graduate without a fall-time offer and be out of a job," I answered.

I let my eyes drift to the left of Silas realized that Dana had been craning her neck to look at us from the living room. When she realized that I caught her looking at us, she gave me a playful smile.

"I'm going to talk with your sister," I said without even thinking about it. Silas raised his eyebrows at me. "Going to find out some dirt on me while she's here?"

"You caught me."

Silas reached out his hand and gently tucked my hair behind my ear. My breath caught at the gesture. He lingered his face close to mine for a beat before heading to the living room, leaving me in the kitchen stunned.

Dana and I sat on two available lawn chairs on the back porch while Silas was being tortured with embarrassing photos by Lisette. Dana had closed the sliding door behind her as we got outside for some added privacy.

"Clara, can I tell you a story?"

I nodded as I sat up in my chair.

"I used to love watching Silas play baseball," Dana spoke with her eyes narrowed, clearly deep in her memories. "There was one game that changed that, though. There he was, on the pitcher's mound, the large number 17 on the back of his uniform. He just finished striking someone out and won his team the game. Everyone was jumping up in victory and celebrating, the spectators all around me extremely excited."

Dana's voice suddenly grew colder. "And yet, Silas stood without so much as a smile on his face. He headed back to the dugout, looking as if this was what he was supposed to do. He didn't see baseball as a sport; it was something that he had to win because that's what his father wanted from him."

"When I made that connection; that Silas got no enjoyment from it, I stopped watching his games. I couldn't take that look of his after every victory; a look that seemed that every victory was in fact a defeat in his heart."

Dana and I sat in silence for a long moment.

"You have no idea how different he's acting than how I remember him," she said somberly, breaking the silence. I looked over at her but waited for her to elaborate.

"Silas was quiet, serious, and always brooding. There was nothing anyone could do that would put a smile on that stubborn boys' face." Dana paused to look over her shoulder at Silas through the sliding door. "And yet I've seen him show more emotion within this past hour than my entire time knowing him."

Dana faced me again, her face a mask hiding any emotions. "He always had this face of someone who had had something ripped away from him, something that they couldn't do anything to get back. I think that something was *you*, Clara. It was always you, even after all of these years."

My heart started to ache, and I placed one of my hands over the other to stop it from trembling. I never imagined Silas would yearn for me year after year. The thought of it formed a question form in my head.

"Did he ever have a girlfriend…?"

"Never. He never dated anyone, Clara," she said decisively. "He always kept to himself and never talked to anyone unless he needed something from them. Him and I got along well enough, and I know that he would have told me if he was ever seeing someone."

Dana suddenly reached out her arm and placed one of her hands over both of mine, and for the first time the trembling I felt came to an end.

"The only thing he ever consistently talked to me about was a girl he had known before he moved away. He never told me your name, but seeing the way he looks at you—eyes he had never shown anyone that I had seen—told me that you had to be."

My eyes drifted down to Dana's hand. I noticed that it was her hand trembling now, not mine. Her hand betrayed her impassive face and her unquivering voice.

"Coming back here invigorated him, Clara. He's more expressive, he's showing his emotions outwardly again. It's something I struggle to do myself, and yet his short time being back brought all of that back for him. The effect you have on him is…certainly something."

"I know this is forward, and I hope you can forgive me, but I need to ask this of you as his sister. I need to know if you feel the same way about him that he does for you."

I watched as Dana's eyes suddenly took on a fierce edge. They took the shape of daggers, sharp enough to cut to bone. At the same time, the shaking in her hand stopped completely.

"If you don't feel the same way, and you are just playing with him, then I'm going to ask that you leave him alone. I don't want him to go through any more suffering. I'd rather he return the way he was before, than watch his heart be torn to pieces."

I felt the intensity from every single word, and knew Dana was speaking straight from her heart. I couldn't help but feel thankful that Silas had someone as passionate as her by his side.

"I—I need to hear everything you've told me from him, until then I don't know exactly how I feel. But," I paused, flashing her a warm smile. "When Silas came back, I was reminded of all of these feelings I had buried deep, deep in my heart. I can tell you that what you've just told me has made me so immensely happy, Dana. And playing with him is something that I could never do," I assured her. Dana softened her features and smiled back at me. "Thank you, Clara."

***

The following day after school, I asked everyone to meet me on the bleachers beside Fall River's baseball field. I knew they'd agree on the fact of wanting to ask me about my mother alone, but I secretly had my own agenda. Lauren and Emmy were with me during my last period, so we made our way over there together.

Ralph was already there waiting for us to arrive. Ralph's expression was more serious than I'd ever seen it, and for some reason there were a few other guys from the baseball team there as well. Silas took longer since he met up with Dana at the front entrance of the school.

"Clara, your mom?" he asked. I smiled at him with appreciation. "Thank you for visiting her the other day. She's doing great, Ralph."

"It's so small and rural compared to what I'm used to back in Arden Bay," Dana remarked as she looked back at Fall River for another look from the bleachers. "But it seems so authentic. I think I could get used to it."

"Authentic is certainly a way to describe it," Ralph answered distractedly, his gaze was fixed solely on Silas. When Silas started to look at him with interest, Ralph refused to look away.

I nudged Lauren's shoulder playfully. "Did you pass on the invitation to Mason, too?" I whispered.

Lauren nudged me back, harder. "Only because you asked." I rolled my eyes at her. "Right, as if it was so out of the way for you."

"They're here," Ralph said craning his neck.

Mason led the way, with Caleb following loosely behind. I knew the truth; he had only come because he felt sorry that my mom had gotten hurt. When our eyes met, I gave him a reassuring smile, one that he didn't return. Things still weren't close to being normal between us, but after his multiple visits to my mother in the hospital, we were at least on speaking terms again.

I had almost missed it, but I noticed Dana discreetly craning her neck and staring at Caleb. Caleb was entirely clueless about it, however.

Everyone settled on the bleachers, leaving me standing alone in front of them. I watched, but didn't say anything, as Dana left Silas's side. Her face was as apathetic as always as she smoothly made her way over and sat down next to Caleb. He seemed to notice and gave her a quick once-over as she sat down. Ralph, on the other hand, didn't seem to notice at all as Emmy made her way through the entire group to take her seat right next to him.

"You guys, thanks for coming and for asking about my mom," I started, nervously. To make matters worse, the additional baseball guys were unexpected additions. I looked at how serious and attentive Silas was looking at me, and it gave me strength. "I spoke to some of you about this before, but I do truly believe that something has happened with this town, and I believe the answer lies in Arden Bay. Take a quick look at this paper."

I pulled out the Arden Bay paper brought by Dana and handed it directly to Caleb. He skimmed the story and handed it off to the next person for inspection.

"More specifically, the answer lies with the reporter that wrote that article, Evelyn Reed." I puffed out my chest and tried to gather all of my resolve. "I'm going to go to Arden Bay and speak to this Evelyn Reed directly. I'm going to ask her about this story she wrote and see what she knows."

Silas gave me an enticing and admiring glance, one that told me he was already supportive of it.

Caleb started to massage his forehead slowly. "Clara, what if you're right? What if there is a reason for everything that's been happening—"

"Just say it already. Just last week we had several stores hit simultaneously. All those businesses took massive losses, and people like Clara's mom got hurt. Add the kidnapping to that, and the forced curfew… are we really pretending we don't know how serious this is?" Ralph interjected.

Caleb sighed. "You're right…But what would you gain from speaking to this Evelyn person? It's not like they're going to tell you anything anyway."

"I need answers," I answered. "I won't find them here; I think I'll find them there."

"She is right about that," Mason said with a humorless whistle. Staying here, just thinking about it all; she isn't going to get to the bottom of anything."

"Bottom of what, exactly?" Caleb asked.

"You really think it's a sort of conspiracy, Clara?" Emmy asked timidly. I looked at her with uncertainty. "Everything's changed ever since I published my feature, and all I did was *insinuate* an increase in crime through a series of disconnected and isolated incidents. I'm forced to do desk work, I don't think I'll be offered a full-time position at my office, and I'm not allowed to get field experience anymore. It can't all be a coincidence."

I paused, fixing my gaze onto Caleb. "If my life is being ruined by something I did, I'm going to get to the bottom of why."

"Besides," I said, struggling to fight back against my rising anger. "I won't overlook this anymore. Not after what happened to my mom."

"You should go," Lauren said suddenly.

Caleb furrowed his brow with worry. "…What if there's trouble?" he asked. I gave Caleb an analytical glance. I could decipher what Caleb was truly saying:

Despite everything that's happened…I don't want anything bad to happen to you, Clara.

"I agree she should go," Mason added as he leaned back on the bleachers. "But you definitely shouldn't go alone. In case Caleb's right and there's trouble."

"That's why I'm going with her," Silas stated with all of the confidence in the world. "The *three* of us are going," Dana corrected.

"You know I'd go with you if you asked me to," Lauren offered. "But I'm not sure I'll be able to do much to help."

"About that," I said as I gave Lauren a concerned

look. "I think you should lay low until I get back. If there really is a conspiracy going on, I want you to be protected. You're credited as being my photographer, so you might be a target, too."

Lauren gave it some thought. "I can stay at my grandparents' house for a few days—until you get back. If anyone comes looking, they'll check my house first." I nodded in agreement.

"What *is* the conspiracy?" Ralph asked grimly. "I know you don't know for certain, but you have to have an idea."

"I think Arden Bay released their prisoners onto Fall River to reduce their incarceration rates in order to secure the funding mentioned in the story," I answered, my voice unwavering. Ralph gave me a shocked look, and the other baseball guys he invited along started murmuring to each other. As if he decided now was the time, Ralph walked down the bleachers and stood right in front of me.

"One of my friends from the team," he paused, tilting his head to the bleachers. One of the baseball guys sat up straighter, and I knew that was who Ralph was referring to. "His father works at the police department here."

I was taken aback but continued to listen closely.

Ralph clenched his fist until his knuckles went white. "My mother was groped and felt up in a general store not too long ago. I've been following the case closely thanks to my friend who's been giving me updates. He managed to get his hands on the security footage of what went down and showed it to me. I've just found out that it was *Silas* that saved my mother from that man that day."

"Silas. You saved my mom. She was helpless and felt powerless against that man. Thank you…" Ralph turned to face him. Silas's eyes were wide in response to the raw emotion in his voice. "I wasn't there to help her, but you stepped in. You didn't even know who she was…Thank you."

Silas's eyes drifted down to the ground beneath Ralphs feet. "She ok?" he asked. "Thanks to you," Ralph answered, relieved.

"Clara," Ralph spoke serious, unsmiling. "Arden Bay can't get away with dumping their prisoners onto my—our—town. I know you feel the same way that I do, after what happened to your mom," he paused, giving me a grim look. I nodded at him, affirming that I understood. If we sat idly by, then *no one* would be safe from these criminals. "You can count on me and all of the guys on the team. Anything you need from us, we'll be there."

Ralph narrowed his eyes at me.

"Bring the story home, Clara. If there's anyone that can do it, it's you."

"There's something else, too," the boy whose father worked at the police department spoke up. "Ralph told me you read about a kidnapping in an advance copy at the library."

I nodded at him, my interest peaked. "I managed to do some digging into that too, while my father was distracted. That kidnapping from over a month ago? The kidnapper is still on the loose and there isn't an ongoing investigation into him anymore. The entire thing was swept under the rug, as if the crime had never occurred at all."

"What? You're saying the police aren't searching for the criminal anymore?" Lauren asked uneasily.

"I've never seen it before but it could mean that...y'know, Fall River cops might be in on whatever is happening, too," the boy answered cautiously.

The group went silent as everyone started giving each other drawn out stares. Mason stirred before breaking the silence at last.

"It's settled, then? You're going after all?" he asked as he got to his feet. I looked over to Caleb one final time. The moment Caleb caught me looking directly at him, he started shaking his head.

"I'm just worried about you. Please don't get yourself into trouble," he murmured.

"I'll be there if she does," Silas said over his shoulder.

"Seriously, Clara," Lauren urged. "Stick together and call us if you need anything."

"Thank you, Ralph—everyone," I said as I looked over at everyone sitting on the bleaches, being supportive and worried. I nodded at them reassuringly.

"I'm going to come back with answers, no matter what."

15

Feeling confident that I packed everything, I finished zipping up my schoolbag and hitched it over my shoulder. Before walking out of the room, I eyed the shoebox sticking out from under my bed. I had opened it several times since the day Silas left town. Each time I did, I pushed it back under my bed with less and less force, until it became permanently visible from beneath the bed.

I opened the box again and impulsively fished out the most important photo from the box, the one of us smiling at the camera. Without a second thought, I placed the photo deep into my bag and left the room without looking back.

When I got to the living room, I stared at the kitchen longingly. I knew that, had my mom been home, she'd have expressed concern over me leaving Fall River.

"Feel bad skipping town without telling your

mom?" Dana asked. I jerked up, startled. I had forgotten that she was waiting for me on my couch.

"…Yeah, I do," I answered. "But she wouldn't have let me, anyway. So what she doesn't know won't hurt her."

"That is, until she is awake, right?" Dana laughed. "Lissette doesn't know I'm leaving, and by the time she does, it'll be too late," I told her.

Silas walked into the house just then, and his eyes lit up as soon as they saw me. "Hey, can I talk to you?"

"Sure," I answered. Dana gave Silas a knowing look and walked over to the kitchen.

"I wanted to give you this," he said as he pulled out a small box wrapped in a messily made bow that I just knew was made by him. "It's an early birthday present."

One of my hands reflexively shot up to my heart. "Silas, my birthday isn't for, like, five months."

"Might prove useful now," he insisted as he extended the box to me. I reached out and unwrapped the bow slowly. I smiled when I saw the new microcassette recorder inside. I've always had to borrow one from my office, and never had one of my own.

"Got it the second I heard you got that part-time job, even before I came to see you," he said, his tone serious. "I had been planning on having it delivered to you this year, even though I hadn't sent you anything for your previous birthdays."

I put the recorder down onto my lap and reached out a hand onto Silas's cheek. I flinched, feeling an almost overpowering desire to pull him into a kiss. Silas didn't so much as move, his eyes watched me unwaveringly.

"This is perfect," I told him, my eyes staring deep into his. "I love it, Silas."

Silas sighed in satisfaction. "Does this make up for the birthdays I missed?"

"Absolutely not," I shot him down. "I'll be expecting presents for each one you missed."

"Figures," he said with a coy smile. "You decided to get me something for this birthday even before deciding to come down yourself?" I asked him.

"Interesting how things work out, right?" he answered. "It's as if I somehow knew I'd be seeing you this year."

Silas gently placed one of his hands the hand I held over his cheek. "With that out of the way, we should get going." He looked behind me at the kitchen before adding, "Right?"

I turned, following his line of sight. I jerked up when I saw Dana peeking over the counter in the kitchen, clearly listening to what was happening. She raised a thumbs-up to signal her approval.

I walked outside and shot Silas's house a final look. I recalled a conversation I had with Lisette the night before.

Lisette was in the kitchen, and I was helping her wash dishes from the dinner we ate as a family. Silas and Dana were talking outside for a minute, so I took advantage and asked Lisette something I had meant to ask for a while.

"Lisette, if you don't mind me asking," I asked nervously. "I've been thinking about Silas's father. Dana told me a little about him, and it got me curious. Can you tell me more about him?"

Lisette dropped the plate she was washing, causing it to break into a million pieces as it shattered on the ground. I rushed to her side, intending to help, but Lisette held up a patient hand, one that said *I got it.*

I left the kitchen and returned a few moments later with a broom in hand. I helped Lisette pick up the fallen pieces by collecting them into the dustpan. It was then that she answered my question.

"Silas's father—Gerald—doesn't love people, Clara. He loves assets. He loves the idea of you, the image of what you contribute to his life. I hesitate to believe that man every truly learned to genuine love something just for the sake of it."

Lisette's movements became stiff as she placed the broom aside, lifting the dustpan and headed to the trashcan. "I divorced him when I realized he doesn't make choices based on emotion. He makes choices based on what gives him the most leverage. That's how he operates."

It was with a careful and precise motion that Lisette dumped the contents of the dustpan into the open trashcan and closed the lid. "I couldn't be with a man like that anymore. So, I left and tried to continue with my life. Like I told you before, I thought I was doing a good thing by leaving Silas with him. He was better off financially, after all. But having Silas back here again made me realize how grave a mistake that truly was."

Lisette was about to continue with the dishes, but I grabbed her arm before she reached over to the faucet. I pulled on it and forced her to face me, pulling her into an embrace. She hugged me back silently.

"I'm so happy you two have each other to count on," she whispered into my ear. Even though I didn't respond, I was sure that she knew I felt the same.

***

I heard the front door close behind myself, bringing my attention back to the present moment. I made sure to lock up, seeing as no one would be back home until I got back.

"Hey, how are we getting to Arden Bay, anyway—" I started to ask as I turned around to face the others.

I cut myself off when I saw Silas's motorcycle parked right in our driveway, two helmets laid out on the seat.

"No…no way…" I stuttered, shaking my head.

"Hey," Silas breathed as he took my hand. "I'll be more careful with you on that bike than if I were carrying a bag full of gold."

Dana sighed, shrugging. "He's right, you know. He's given me a few rides, and he outright refused to go faster than the speed limit when he had me with him, even when I begged him to let me feel the wind."

"If I wanted to go fast, I'd go to a track," Silas said, unflinching. "And besides, we'd have more mobility this way than having to stick to public transportation over there."

"What about you, Dana? How are you getting back to town?"

"There's a bus that takes you there without any stops. We could all take it, but when we got there, you wouldn't have any wheels. It's better if you two go there on the bike so that you could move around easily in town."

"Wait…Couldn't I go with you on the bus instead?"

"Clara, I seriously think you'll like it," Silas insisted.

I took a deep breath, feeling all the fight I had left whisked away as I exhaled. It wasn't that I didn't trust Silas, it's just that I was afraid of riding on the bike. It may be true that I had always found biker guys attractive, but I never for a second wanted to be riding on one.

"Ok," I gave in. Silas made one final look at his house.

"Lisette told me her door is always open if I wanted to stay," Dana said longingly. I looked over at her, surprised. "This is a beautiful town, and everyone's been really nice. But I couldn't leave my mother alone."

I realized with a start that I never asked Dana what her mother was like. I made a mental note to ask her all about her at the next opportunity I got.

"We all love you, Dana," I told her. "I know we're seeing each other in Arden Bay, but you should come back soon." Dana looked at me with the smallest yet gentlest smile on her face. Dana walked around me and started tying my hair with a hair tie she had banded around her wrist. "Low ponytails are the best for when

Silas puts the helmet on your head." I quietly let Dana tie my hair, feeling closer to her than I ever felt. Never before had I felt that familial bond of two sisters, and yet I thought what I felt for Dana must have been something similar. When she was finished, I looked at her and felt confident that I could call her my sister one day.

"Ready to go?" Silas asked. I nodded at him, trying to hide my nervousness.

Silas lifted up a helmet and placed it over my head, careful not to hurt me in the process. "You know, I originally bought this helmet for you in mind," he said. "Emmy just happened to wear it before you."

I immediately started blushing, remembering the jealousy I felt when I realized it was Emmy riding on the back of Silas's motorcycle. It felt like such a long time ago now.

With his helmet on his head, Silas mounted the bike first. He kicked up the kickstand and placed both of his feet firmly on the ground, tilting his helmet as a means of indicating that I had to get on now.

Silas had parked the bike in a way so that I could approach from the left side. I learned why when I saw a footpeg on the left side of the bike. I placed my left foot on the small footpeg and hesitated, afraid the bike might tip. And yet the bike felt solid.

Silas looked to the side, and I could see him watching me from his rearview mirror. Seeing his encouraging eyes gave me the motivation to fight through my fears. I placed my left hand on his shoulder and lifted my right leg high, arching it over the bike's rear fender. The seat itself was thin and somewhat uncomfortable.

However, the seat's comfort was not the most prominent thing I felt. As soon as I settled into the seat, my hips instinctively slid forward, inching me ever closer to Silas. Before long, my hips were in direct contact with his back.

"I need you as close as possible to me, for safety," I heard Silas instruct me through his helmet. Thankful that my helmet was covering up how red my cheeks and ears had gotten, I squeezed my knees against his thighs. I wrapped my arms securely around his waist.

Silas lifted his visor for a brief moment and looked over at Dana one last time.

"We're getting to the bottom of this," he said to her. I looked over at Dana as a range of emotions flashed through her eyes. Her and Silas seemed to have an entire conversation with their silent looks; a language that could be deciphered from them alone.

"Love you," he called out to her as if bringing an end to the exchange. He closed his helmet's visor and faced forward again. The emotionless mask Dana used to hide her true feelings betrayed her, as her surprise was as clear as day

"Love you too," she called back.

I saw Silas turn the key to the ignition. He pressed the start button and the engine beneath me roared to life with a loud, mechanical sound. Silas slightly twisted the throttle, and it increased the engine's pitch, making the sound grow sharper.

Silas looked at me from the rearview mirror one last

time. I knew he was waiting for one last nonverbal confirmation before setting off. I did a quick checklist of the things I brought in my bag, and made sure my sanity was still in check. Then I squeezed Silas's sides, the simplest way I could think of to communicate my readiness.

Right afterwards, Silas did something and I felt distinct clunk as the motorcycle began to creep forward. Just before they were no longer in sight, I turned to see Dana on the sidewalk. I etched the sight to memory, feeling a strange pain in my chest I couldn't quite explain.

16

It took me a few moments to process the fact that I was so much higher than Silas was. Sitting on the passenger seat of the bike, I was perched up and over him, giving me a clear view of the back of his helmet and a terrifying, exposed view of the road ahead. I felt like I was riding on a pedestal, unstable and separate from him in a way I hadn't expected. The position forced me to cling to him, my arms wrapped around his waist, my chest pressed against his back. It was a physical reminder of my vulnerable position and how completely I was relying on him to be my anchor.

The noise and wind were relentless. Even with the helmet, the engine's constant growl vibrated through my bones, a deep, mechanical hum that settled into my chest. But the wind was what truly dominated my senses, a loud and powerful presence that pushed against my body. It pressed my cheeks against the inside of the helmet and whipped at my clothes.

Just like Dana had said, it was obvious how mindful Silas was of his speed and was refusing to accelerate too far. I could tell by his speed relative to the cars around us. And yet the wind made it feel like we were moving even faster than we were.

In that small, vibrating world, my fear began to morph into something else. I wasn't just holding on to him; I was being held. His body moved with confidence, and I followed, trusting him completely. The turns were albeit still a little scary, my body wanting to stay upright, but his solid form guided me, pulling me along in a synchronized dance. I could feel the tension in his muscles, the subtle adjustments he made to keep us safe, and I realized that my terror was being absorbed by his expertise. My fear became a memory, fading with every beat of his heart against my own. This wasn't a scary journey anymore, it was a moment of quiet connection, a secret understood between the two of us.

I looked over his helmet and onto the road in front of us. In that moment, I felt like we could take on the entire world.

***

Our first stop was at the same gas station that Silas stopped at between Arden Bay and Fall River. Silas had gotten gas before the trip started, so we covered quite a bit of ground.

Just like when I had been getting on the bike, Silas

waited for me to dismount first while he waited and stabilized the motorcycle. I carefully swung my leg back over to the left side again. When my feet were back on solid ground again, it instantly felt strange to me. Silas hadn't been looking at me when it happened, but I almost tripped over nothing and fell over. Thankfully, I caught myself before it happened.

"How are you feeling?" Silas asked me as he removed the helmet over my head, something that by that point I felt was a part of myself. I blinked multiple times, feeling sensory overload as I suddenly felt something that wasn't the strong wind and engine noises.

When I looked at Silas, though, the thing that I felt the most was an immense sense of accomplishment and relief. I had faced my fears and not only survived but got to share something with Silas. He tilted his head at me, confused.

"You okay—" Silas started to ask, but I swiftly cut him off with a hug. I buried my head into his chest wordlessly. Clearly caught off guard, Silas dropped my helmet to the ground. His arms were wrapped around me in seconds.

I pulled away from him quickly, looking at my helmet on the floor. "First the paper I had in my hands and now this…Looks like we keep dropping things," I looked up at him teasingly. "Can't imagine why," he answered with a seductive smile.

Taking a deep breath, I looked around the gas station. It was the same one that Silas found trouble in last time he was here. And yet, like I suspected, there wasn't anyone around.

"You want to come with while I pay inside?" Silas asked, reading my mind. I nodded in agreement, and we walked into the gas station together.

Just as I started to wonder if the gas station employee would recognize Silas, I saw an expression of dread appear on the employee's face. "It's you again…" he trailed off.

Silas raised both of his hands in the air playfully. "Hey, hey, I was worried about an innocent couple getting gas. What's with the hate?" The employee shook his head. "What pump are you? Please, just get out of here."

After a quick scan to make sure there wasn't anyone else in the store, I approached the counter. "Did something happen after that fight happened? Is that why you're annoyed?"

The employee eyed me closely. Just as I suspected, he started talking. A part of me suspected he wouldn't have answered if it was Silas asking the same question.

"You have no idea the yellow tape I had to deal with after he left. The second that fight was over, *this guy* got right on his bike and left, leaving me alone to handle everything."

Silas narrowed his eyes at him. "You're the one that should've intervened. I did because no one else did. Besides, of course you had to deal with the aftermath; you work here."

"Wait, I'm confused," I cut in. "What yellow tape are you taking about? No one died, did they?"

The employee gave me an apprehensive look before

answering. "When the cops showed up, they put yellow tape everywhere and waited for other cops to show up. It wasn't as simple as them getting arrested and calling it a day. It all happened so fast, but it looked like they wanted the situation handled a certain way."

Silas and I exchanged confused glances. The employee suddenly sat back on his chair. "Come to think of it, I had been told to contact the cops if you ever came back here," he said nonchalantly.

I felt the entire store go still. Even though I couldn't see him, I could feel Silas tensing up, considering different courses of action.

"No, no, don't worry, I don't want to deal with all that yellow tape again," he added hastily. "Strange part is, I was told to call this number instead of the cops directly," he said as he handed over a sheet of paper he had stashed near the cash register. I looked at the phone number on the paper. I took out my own notebook to copy the number down.

"Keep it," the employee said instantly. "Like I said, I don't want to deal with those people again. They were pushy."

"You sure they were law enforcement?" Silas asked hesitantly.

"They had uniforms, badges, guns…everything. Yeah, those were cops."

Silas shifted next to me, his hands digging deeper into his pockets. "Any chance the other cops that showed up belong to Arden Bay?"

The employee thought about it for a beat. "Could be…I'm not sure."

I placed the sheet of paper inside of my notebook and secured it in my bag. I was deep in my thoughts as Silas filled the motorcycle's gas tank. That's when an idea suddenly popped into my head. I shrugged off my bag from my shoulder, and I opened my notebook.

"I had a feeling," I said with an ominous feeling crawling over my skin. "What's up?" Silas asked as he closed the fuel cap on the bike.

"It's the area code, Silas. I had written down Arden Bay's area code before we came." I looked up from the notebook and met Silas's gaze. "It's the same. This phone number has the same area code as Arden Bay."

"I could've told you that much," Silas said sheepishly. I gave him a look. "You never asked," he said, raising his hands innocently.

Silas's expression grew serious. "Those had to have been Arden Bay investigators. Yet another trail that leads back to there," he said.

"How deep does this go," I asked him, concerned. "You considering backing out?" he asked.

I placed a hand on my hip and gave him a look. "As if," I answered coldly. "I told you…I'm not going back without answers."

Silas approached me and bent over at the waist slightly so were stood eye-to-eye.

"I had a feeling you'd say that," he breathed.

17

Silas brought the bike to a gentle and slow stop on the side of the road. I felt much more comfortable kicking my leg over to get off the bike. Silas looked up at the sky pensively. With one smooth movement, he kicked down his kickstand and got off the bike too.

"We'll start up again when the sky clears up," he says patiently. I nodded at him, trusting in his judgement.

It had begun to rain softly, and the sky started getting darker, indicating the rain would soon get much worse. Silas spotted an overpass and stopped under it so that we could have some shelter from the rain. It wasn't five minutes after Silas chose to stop that it began to pour with an intensity that I hadn't seen in some time.

"Whew, dodged a bullet there," Silas said looking at the downpour. I felt a chill and tried to nonchalantly cozy up to him for warmth. Silas didn't hesitate for even a second; he immediately took off his jacket and draped it over my shoulders. I couldn't contain the grin on my face as I felt like a princess being offered a coat by her prince.

Silas and I took to watching the cars pass silently. "I wouldn't change a thing, you know," I told him quietly. Even though riding the bike forced us to stop, I wanted Silas to know I wouldn't have changed a thing. Silas reached out with a gentle hand and placed it on the top of my head, a gesture I couldn't help but love.

It was then that I thought of a question. "Silas, why didn't you want to tell me the reasons behind your fights? The one at the gas station and the one that involved Ralph's mom?"

I caught a shy look in Silas's eye at the question. He massaged the back of his neck before answering. "I was kind of trying to make you think I was a bit of…trouble." I tiled my head to the side, lost. "Huh?"

"It's been four years since you last saw me, so I decided that I wanted to look dangerous to you. I thought that might make it more likely that you'd, you know…think that I was hot, or something."

Silas's ears had reddened significantly as he admitted the truth. "You were trying to keep up appearances? To make it seem like you were getting into fights because you were a bad boy?"

"Oh, please don't describe it that way—"

I leaned in close to Silas, a playful grin on my face. "I thought you were hot from your motorcycle alone, you know." I narrowed my eyes even further. "And no amount of pretending that you were dangerous would have kept me away from you, by the way."

"Guess the motorcycle served its purpose," Silas answered, leaning away from me with an embarrassed look. It was a look I couldn't get enough of.

Just then, another question came to my mind. "Hey, Dana told me something that I wanted to ask you about…"

"Oh, man. Now you have me worried," he said nervously. I pushed him with my shoulder playfully.

"If you don't want to talk about it, I'd get it. It's just—" I coughed, trying to get to the point. "Is it true you never had a girlfriend? The entire time, since you've left?"

Silas took a deep breath. He leaned into me slightly, giving me the impression that he was borrowing from my strength to be able to say the answer. "That day when I left town again, and I said that I never stopped thinking about you?" Silas asked. I blinked towards the ground, my cheeks burning. "That wasn't a lie," he said affectionately. "I never had eyes for anyone else."

I opened my mouth to say something, but he placed his hand gently over my mouth. "I sort of got into the motions these past four years. Time went by but I never felt like I was truly living my life. I would constantly think back to my time in Fall River and when you were in my life."

My eyes widened as I stared at Silas. Even if he lowered his hand from my mouth, I wouldn't know what to say.

"You kept me going, Clara. I would run away to you

in my mind. Even when I played baseball; it all felt pointless. I could feel myself detaching from the moment and pretending you were there, so that I'd have a reason to do things; anything," Silas's eyes drifted downwards, as if he was reliving what he was describing.

Realizing how depressed he sounded, Silas jerked upwards. "Don't get the wrong idea—I was moving on in my own way. I knew that life moves on, and that I couldn't live in the past forever. That was one of the reasons I came back to town, you know. I wanted to see for myself if it was pointless living in the past, and if it was time for me to start focusing on the future."

Silas started massaging the back of his neck. "That's why I knew it was too good to be true when I got here and you had a boyfriend. I totally understood, then. That was reality. I never called or even wrote. How could you possibly have waited for me all that time?"

I did, Silas. A piece of my heart always did wait for you, somehow. Even after all this time.

The week that we wrote letters to each other immediately flashed in my mind, and I knew that it did Silas's as well. "I considered it, you know. Writing you. But I was always afraid to learn that you'd found someone else. So, I never did."

"Being with you ever since I got back has felt like a dream, like at any time I'm just going to wake up, and I'd be back in my room at my dad's house," he chuckled ominously as he lowered his hand slowly from my mouth. I caught his hand with mine while it was still within my reach.

"I built up all sorts of ideas about what it'd be like if you came back; I never expected it would happen the way it did at the farmers' market. Sometimes I felt like you being back is a dream…What if it is, Silas?" I asked, my tone even.

Silas looked at me analytically. "If it is, then I never want to wake up," he exhaled heavily.

"I really wish you'd have written. It'd have made things much easier, you know."

"The feeling's mutual. But you do know writing letters is a two-way street, *Ms. Reporter.* You could have written me, too."

***

"Hm?"

"What's up?" Silas asked me. "Since when has that guy been sitting there?" I asked, noticing a stranger sitting under the underpass in the distance, off to our side.

"I never noticed he was there," Silas answered. Something about the man caught my attention. I had been looking in that direction just a moment earlier, and yet I never noticed anyone sitting there.

"Silas, can you stay here? I'm going to talk to him." I thought Silas might refuse, yet he didn't stop me at all. He held my back comfortingly for a moment until I started to walk towards the stranger.

I approached the man, and something immediately caught my attention about him. I looked up at the sky just beyond the underpass. The rain was still coming down, hard, and there was no vehicle next to the stranger. Despite that, the man was completely dry.

The stranger sat on the ground, head bowed, seeming oblivious to me approaching him. His clothing was an expanse of darkest black, but not a dull black. It was a rich, textured set of clothes from a different time period. He wore layers of heavy fabric, intricate straps, and perhaps a hint of leather. It was like looking at a silhouette of a different world, an almost gothic appearance that didn't belong.

I stood just above the man, staring down at him as if waiting him to take notice of me. He sat with his head uncovered, and I could see his pure black hair. It was a mess of curls, and just like his clothing, his hair wasn't wet in the slightest.

He remained motionless, his gaze refusing to leave the ground, even as he began to speak to me.

"What's your name?"

"Clara," I answered without hesitation.

"Your journey, what is the purpose behind it?"

I was confused by the question and yet understood the meaning behind it almost as quickly as he asked it.

"I want to understand if I belong. Getting to the truth about my town…I need to do this to prove myself and make everyone safe."

"And if you're wrong— If you fail, and you not only fail to save everyone, but find out that you don't belong? What will you do then?"

I stared at the stranger. Upon closer inspection, it wasn't so much a man but a guy just a few years older than me. He gave the impression of someone who has aged beyond his years and has been weathered like a rock against the never-ending crashing of a shoreline.

"Then I will work harder. I'll work harder until I do belong—until I can prove that I'm enough."

The young man flinched when he heard my words. His head tilted up ever so slightly.

"You wouldn't give up?"

"If this were something that I could just give up over after failing the first time, then it wouldn't have been worth pursuing in the first place."

I couldn't exactly tell from my angle, but I thought I caught a glimpse of a smile on the stranger's face.

Without another word, he reached beneath the layers of fabric and pulled out a single rusted coin. He flicked the coin in the air and caught it carefully. He then slowly opened it and peered at it within his palm. He didn't present it to me nor say anything more about it. He simply put the coin back into the fabric.

"I hope you find the answer you were looking for, Clara," he said, slightly more emotive than he had spoken anything else before.

"One last thing," the young man began to say resolutely. "If you had to choose between finding the answer you seek and that boy you left behind, which would you choose?"

I turned to look at Silas off in the distance. He realized I was watching him, and he gave me a gentle wave.

I smiled and waved at him. Confident that I knew the answer to the question, I turned, prepared to tell the young man my response.

I stared, confused, as the floor beneath my feet was empty. There was no one around at all, and try as I might, I couldn't remember why I had walked over to this spot at all. I looked over at Silas and blinked at him several times, wondering why I'd wandered so far away from him.

I jogged back to return to Silas's side, my mind racing. I opened my mouth to ask Silas what I was doing on the opposite side of the underpass, and yet the question disappeared from my mind. Silas continued to look at the falling rain, and I took to staring in the same direction as he was. I rested my head against his shoulder, immensely happy to be by his side again.

18

As the immense city of Arden Bay came into view, I tightened my grip on Silas's waist. I got the irresistible feeling that answers were ahead. The tall, looming buildings overhead were nothing less than grim reminders that this was nothing like the small, homey town I left behind. My only sense of comfort was the boy sitting right in front of me, someone who I had no intention of letting go of.

And yet, once we crossed into the city, I couldn't help but admire the large industrial city. Watching the city from the back of a motorcycle was an entirely new experience on its own. Silas weaved through the buildings, and I helped him lean in during the turns. We rode past massive warehouses and vast parking lots that seemed to be waiting for something new.

As we neared the core, we reached an elevated highway, the city's skyline opened up before us. The sun was starting to set, and the first of the city's neon signs blinked on. Of all the signs, there was one giant, glowing sign in the distance that drew my eyes. The red triangle and blue letters pulsed over the jumble of large buildings, a familiar and reassuring sign that we were almost there.

The concrete lanes gave way to narrower, cobblestone streets. On the sidewalks, people moved in a bustling flow. College students walked freely as we drove past a string of university buildings, people in business suits, kids on skateboards, all rushed along with purpose.

I was so distracted admiring the city that I didn't realize when we came to a stop and Silas killed the ignition. He was staring at me patiently through his rearview mirror. Embarrassed, I got off the bike and waited for him to help me take off my helmet.

"It really didn't feel like a three-and-a-half-hour trip," I told him. Silas removed his own helmet. "We were held back by the rain, but I agree," he paused, giving me a flirtatious smile. "Having your arms around me made the hours fly by. If only you were with me during my ride to Fall River."

"I'd ride with you on a long road trip," I said, feeling shy right after I said the words. "I—I mean, if you wanted to…"

"I'm already planning it in my head," Silas answered instantly. I tried to act nonchalant at the prospect of going on another ride with Silas. Hopefully, this next ride won't involve trying to solve some conspiracy.

Once we gathered all of our things, I turned to see

where we arrived at. The strap of my school bag almost slid completely off of my shoulder.

"Sorry that it isn't a major chain. Popular and high-end hotels wouldn't have given me a room since I'm not over 21. I called ahead and this is an independent motel. They'll give me the room even though I'm 18," he said nonchalantly. He held his helmet under his arm and my helmet in his free hand as he started to walk towards the motel entrance.

I gulped, hard, as I stared at the motel. It definitely was small, and it was obvious that it was independently run from a larger chain.

And yet it wasn't the motel that kept me rooted to the spot, afraid to take a step. Whether it be my naivety or ignorance, it was the first time that I truly realized that Silas and I were going to sleep, alone, in a motel in an entirely different city.

What were his expectations? I couldn't help but wonder. Something had to happen, right? He's expecting it to. What if I'm not ready? What if I disappoint him? What if—

"Hey," Silas murmured, leaning close. He lifted my trembling hand and pressed it against his chest. "Clara, I didn't book this to get you alone with me. If you aren't comfortable with it, we could go somewhere else. The only reason didn't take you to my house is because that'd defeat the purpose of our plan. My parents can't see us together just yet so that you could be allowed into The Town Local."

I peered at his unwavering, sincere eyes. My trembling hand found comfort not only in his hand but also from his rapidly beating heart, which I could feel through his shirt.

You're nervous about this, too, aren't you?

I smiled at him, feeling a thundering in my chest, and yet I felt much calmer than I did just a moment earlier. "Thanks, Silas. I'm fine, let's go," I told him. He let me hand drop to my side, and yet I had the lingering desire that he'd continue to hold it for just a minute longer. I focused my eyes on his hand as we walked towards the entrance.

Silas approached the front desk and asked me to wait in the lobby. When he was done, he returned to get me. "Our room is this way," he said. He gave me a look of slight concern. "Clara, I had to pay cash for the room up front. I didn't have enough cash for two rooms, I hope that's alright."

I shook my head at him profusely. "No—no, I wouldn't have wanted you to spend more money than you had to," I said, and yet my mind was going fuzzy with all sorts of thoughts.

Truth was, it was obvious that we were both overlooking one simple thing: I couldn't go to Silas's house because of our plan, but that wasn't stopping *Silas* from going home and letting me stay in the room alone. We both knew it, and yet we had a nonverbal agreement to overlook that simple fact altogether.

We're both desperate to be alone. My heart knew that was the answer before my mind did.

The elevator ride was an uncomfortably silent one as Silas led the way to our room. Silas inserted the metal key into the doorknob and opened the door for me, waiting for me to walk inside. Somehow, I already expected the room to have a single bed before walking inside. And yet the sight of it still made my cheeks and ears hot.

"You should shower first," Silas said, surprising me. I hadn't realize I had just been standing in the center of the room, lost in thought. "Oh—right, I'll go first," I answered mechanically. I placed my bag on the bed and fished out my clothes. I walked into the bathroom and felt the strength of my legs give out. I looked at my reflection in the mirror and tried to slap both of my cheeks resolutely, trying to calm myself down.

I showered and changed into baggy clothes that I usually sleep in. I didn't want to keep Silas waiting, so I hurried as much as I could. The moment I left the bathroom and made eye contact with Silas, I froze in place as I saw the look he had in his eyes, a look like he was entirely captivated by me. He was organizing something in his bag, and yet when he laid his eyes on me it seemed like I made him lose his train of thought.

"Right, I'll go next," Silas said, realizing he was hadn't moved for multiple moments. He silently gathered his clothes and stopped right in front of me before reaching the bathroom.

"This how you always look before going to bed?" he asked.

I nodded, looking up at him shyly.

"Just dedicated it to memory. Too hard to resist."

He grabbed the door handle of the bathroom, yet he paused when he heard what I had to say next.

"Why dedicate it to memory when this won't be the

last time you see it?" I almost whispered.

Silas didn't look back at me before closing the bathroom door behind him. The strength in my legs gave out as I threw myself onto the bed, burying my head in the pillows. There was no point in trying to stop my nerves.

I blinked, hearing words Silas said during that birthday of mine before he moved away coming back to me.

This flower reminds me of you, he had said. He was unable to meet my eyes as he nervously gave me the yellow flower I kept in the shoebox beneath my bed.

I sat up and reached out to grab my bag. I pulled out the photo of me standing beside him. I had shoved it into my bag without thinking much of it, and yet I was thankful that I had.

Growing curious, I looked over at the bag Silas left behind. I knew it was wrong, but I was looking for absolutely anything to distract my increasingly impure thoughts. My breath caught as I noticed the unopened pack of condoms—but there was something else in the bag that drew my eyes even more.

It was with trembling fingers that I pulled out a laminated photo of myself looking at the camera with a cute smile, a radiant and lovely look in my eyes. I remember that it was a photo taken by Silas himself all of those years ago, the look in my eyes dedicated to the boy behind the camera. I never knew he kept the photo, and that he went as far as to laminate it. It was in pristine condition, as if it meant the world to him to keep it safe.

My eyes narrowed, tears starting to form in the corner of my eyes.

All of those years ago, I lost someone so important to me.

I hardly reacted as Silas opened the bathroom door and immediately dropped the towel he was using to dry his hair when he saw me. He approached me slowly, as if he was afraid I would wither away if he moved too quickly. He kneeled in front of me, wiping away the tears forming in my eyes. The fact that he was shirtless didn't garner a reaction from me, either.

How badly did I want to see you again. Daily, I yearned to see you face, to hear your voice.

Silas gently grabbed the photos from my fingers; the one I brought with me, and the one I found in his bag. He gave them a passing glance, as if to confirm his suspicions of what the two photos were. His eyes lingered slightly longer on the picture of the two of us.

I built walls around my heart to protect myself from the fact that you were gone, and that I might never see you again. But now that you're here, Silas, I'm afraid those walls have been brought down and cannot be put back up again.

With careful hands, Silas placed the photos on the table beside the bed. He carefully placed our picture on top, taking great care to prevent me from seeing the back of the photo he had of me. I reached out a soft hand and gently ran my fingers through his hair.

You are one of a kind, Silas Quinn. And I would have spent a lifetime waiting for you if it had meant I got to see you again.

My hand ran down the side of his face, and Silas quickly reached up a hand to stop my hand from leaving his cheek. He started to kiss my hand as softly as a mother does her newborn: loving, gently, with no secrets.

It couldn't be clearer to me now how badly in love with you I was. I was in love with you then, and I've managed to fall for you all over again.

Silas pushed me gently against the bed. He supported his weight with both of his hands, as if worried about hurting me by putting his entire body weight on me. I smiled despite myself.

Even at a time like this, you worry about something like that? You truly are a gentleman, aren't you?

Silas looked at me with a hungry, almost desperate look in his eyes. The thought that he wanted me, needed me, made my breath catch.

"…Clara?"

The word came out so quietly that if I hadn't given him my undivided attention, I'd have missed it. His eyes trembled in fear, and I admired him for asking before moving any farther.

"Yes, Silas?" I answered temptingly. His eyes became alive with electricity, and I could almost visibly see his hormonal urges surging through to new heights.

"Is this…ok?" he asked in a throaty whisper. Silas sounded as if it was taking every fiber of his being to hold himself back, his sanity hanging on a mere thread that dangled on my fingertips. The thought excited me more than anything in my entire life.

I brought up my hands and dragged them through his body, teasingly. I couldn't help but play with him, knowing there was a leash keeping him right where he was. I knew that he wouldn't dare move without telling him to.

Silly boy. Don't you know, Silas?

The heavy panting that escaped his mouth felt warm as it reached my face. I could see his eyes glazing over as he tried to regain his focus.

Don't you know that I want you? The same way you want me…if not more?

"Come here already," I breathed. I reached out and pulled Silas into a deep, passionate kiss. Silas made a sound of pure pleasure, but I barely even registered the sound. The bed beneath me felt as if it had disappeared as my lips pressed against Silas's. He took a moment to even move, as if he was afraid that moving at all would bring the moment to an end. Eventually he tilted his head the other way, bringing the briefest pause to our kiss. The pause filled me with longing, and I reached out, desperate for more. Silas reciprocated, and his lips found mine again. His hands started to travel throughout my body, making their way down to my waist, then to my hips…

"It feels—" Silas purred as the last bit of restraint left his body. "…It feels like I've waiting my entire life for this moment."

His hands traveled even further, and the world beyond the room ceased to exist.

There was only Silas.

19

I opened my bag and pulled out the notes I had prepared beforehand. I started looking over them, making sure I didn't miss anything. I tried to find a comfortable position, but the motel lobby couches weren't doing me any favors.

Silas returned from the front desk. "We're good to go, but no rush. Let me know when you're ready," he said.

"Mm," I answered airily. Ever since I woke up that morning, it had been impossible to look Silas directly in the eyes. The thought of it alone made me feel butterflies in my stomach. As Silas passed by me on the couch, he was careful to avoid touching me in the slightest.

I widened my eyes, realizing that he might be thinking that I wanted to create some distance between us after what happened last night. I reached out my hand and grabbed his wrist before he was out of reach.

He looked at me with a tinge of surprise in his eyes, confirming my suspicion. I tilted my chin up at him, knowing he'd take the hint. He was hesitant at first, but eventually he bent at the waist slowly, giving me a kiss on my lips.

Today was the day I was going to visit Evelyn Reed, the reporter behind the feature Dana showed me. Feeling confident I had everything I needed in my notebook, I put everything back in my bag and got to my feet. Silas did the same and we headed out towards his bike.

"One sec, I'm going to call Dana so that she can meet us at The Town Local," Silas told me before heading back to the front desk. I watched as the employee offered Silas a landline he could borrow. The phone call was quick, and he rejoined me shortly after. Silas nodded at me before we left. "She'll be there," he said.

It felt great to be on road again, my arms hugging Silas's sides tight. Despite riding behind Silas on the same motorcycle as the previous day, I felt closer to him than ever before. It felt like the bond between us couldn't be broken. The distance that had been built between us after those four years apart had been bridged with an untearable material. Silas could no longer be *someone that I used to know*, anymore.

I was hoping to be more mentally prepared by the time we arrived, and yet I was nowhere near as confident as I thought I'd be when Silas killed the ignition. I looked around us, confused.

"Where is it?" I asked. "This is the parking lot, Clara. Evelyn's in there," Silas pointed to the large building looming over us. It was the largest building of those around us, and it cast an immense shadow right over us.

Silas waited patiently for me to get off the bike first before moving. Once he got my helmet off, he removed his own and lingered by the bike.

I took another long at the building ahead of us. It seemed to bend towards me, taunting me.

"I know I'm going to go in alone, at least at first. But I really wished you'd be going in with me."

Silas made a strained face. "Trust me. It's as hard as it is for me to hold back and let you go in first as it is for you to go in alone."

"Walk me through the plan again," I insisted.

"I'm going to follow you up to the entrance. When you manage to find out what floor Evelyn's at, I want you to tell me by holding up your fingers behind yourself. Then, I can follow behind you and go to that floor to back you up. There are too many floors in that building to go wandering around aimlessly."

Silas noticed my hesitation. "Clara, you won't be in there alone for long," he said comfortingly.

I nodded silently at him, finding comfort in his reassuring eyes.

"Dana?" I asked. "Don't worry about her. She'll be here; you just focus on telling me what floor."

I walked into the building first, Silas lingering outside of the door. Walking in alone felt lonely, but I tried my best to steel my resolve. I gripped the bag over my shoulder tighter as I approached the front desk.

"Hi, I'm looking for The Town Local?" I asked the security guard sitting behind the counter. He gave me a once over. "You got clearance? Someone ask you to come?" he asked gruffly.

"Yes, Evelyn Reed, community reporter," I answered immediately.

"Who're you?" he asked.

"I'm an aspiring reporter, and I've temped for Evelyn before. There was something I wanted to ask her, it shouldn't take long."

The guard didn't move for a long time as he judged me silently. Yet I didn't so much as flinch. I wasn't leaving this building without answers. Without a word, he picked up a phone on his desk and turned away from the desk for privacy. He spoke onto the phone for a bit, looking over at me a couple of times.

I swallowed, refusing to look away from the guard even once. Once he hung up the phone, he jerked his head to the left.

"Tenth floor," is all he said. I nodded at him and turned to it as nonchalantly. I made a silent prayer that Silas was still looking at me as I held five fingers up behind me. I then closed my fist and extended all five of my fingers again to signal that I meant ten. My fingers were trembling too hard for me to press the call button, so I had to take a deep, calming breath before I could press the button.

Once the elevator doors closed, I bent over and had my hands over my knees. I'd never told a lie like that, and I felt proud but exasperated. Whether the guard caught my bluff or not, it wasn't clear. I was just happy to have gotten this far.

The doors opened and I laid eyes on The Town Local for the first time.

Describing The Town Local as the polar opposite of the local paper at Fall River would be an understatement and at the same time an insult to The Town Local. I walked into absolute madness: reporters tripping over themselves speaking into phones like madmen requesting leads, editors arguing with other editors and their bosses regarding the latest issue, the rhythmic clatter of computer keyboards ear-splittingly constant, and fax machines working almost non-stop.

Despite the overwhelming movement, it was truly a controlled chaos. Everyone knew the general flow and not a single person looked out of place. I couldn't help but admire it all, wondering if I could ever make it in the local paper for a big city like Arden Bay.

"Visitor, what do you want?" a man approached me on a swivel chair, not bothering to get up to his feet.

"I—I'm looking for Evelyn Reed?" I stammered. "Sorry?" the guy asked, and I repeated myself. He looked at me for a beat, confused.

Suddenly, the guy pushed himself back to his desk with a kick. He stayed in his seat as he pulled out the phone on his desk and talked to it briefly before hanging it up. He never acknowledged me again.

I looked at the office again, realizing that it was so massive that it was easier for this guy to call Evelyn on the phone to reach her as opposed to calling out her name.

"Visitor," a woman's voice called out from my right. I turned to see the woman in front of me. My first thought when I saw Evelyn was that she was beautiful. Her hair was cut into a chin-length bob, a bob cut with exceptional precision. All the lines in her face, hair, even clothes were perfectly straight, showing no sign of softness.

The longer I stared at Evelyn, the clearer it became that she had an icy, predatory presence. Her eyes were gray, lacking any warmth. They looked at me with a constant, calculating judgement. It was almost enough for me to walk back towards the elevator.

And yet that wasn't an option. It never was.

Evelyn didn't add anything else after *visitor*, so I started talking instead. "Hello, it's nice to meet you. I was hoping we could have a quick moment to talk. My name is Clara Monroe, part-time reporter working for the Fall River local paper."

She listened to me with a disinterested look, but when I said my name and brought up Fall River, I noticed a change in her expression. Her eyes changed to analyze me for seemingly the first time.

"My office," is all she said as she turned around and walked further into the floor.

I hadn't realized that Evelyn was high up enough to have her own office, but deep within The Town Local she had her own spacious office. She closed the door after I walked in. There was a single chair for someone to sit in that wasn't Evelyns chair behind her desk. I smiled nervously at Evelyn as I sat down.

"You must think you're pretty clever, lying to get up

here," Evelyn said coldly before she even finished sitting down. I chuckled nervously, the only way I could think to respond.

"What can I do for you?"

I took a deep breath before starting. "Evelyn, the reason of my visit is the feature you wrote, titled A Beacon of Progress."

One of Evelyns' eyebrows shot up for a brief second as she heard the title. I knew she would recognize what I meant. Like any reporter, I knew that we took great pride in our work and would recognize it from hearing the title alone.

"Evelyn, you see, just before you published this story, I wrote a feature that somewhat contradicts what's written in A Beacon of Progress. I mentioned how—"

I froze, unsure about how to refer Silas by. Calling him an acquaintance couldn't be further from the truth and calling him a friend didn't feel right either.

"My boyfriend, Silas, had experienced a crime-related activity in a gas station between our two towns, and finally inside our own town as well."

Evelyn made a face. She rolled her shoulders back and craned her neck to the side in a half-hearted attempt to crack it. "I don't see how that's a contradiction to what I wrote in my story," Evelyn said coldly.

"Your story mentions a 28% decrease in average inmate count," I read out with a quick look at my notebook on my lap, "That occurred just on time to receive $12.5 million in additional funding for the city."

"That's what's written in my feature, thank you for reading it back to me," Evelyn droned. I held strong and didn't let it bother me.

"What I consider to be the contradiction, Evelyn, is how you mention in your story that this decrease in inmate count was thanks to a unique solution to an escalating problem. And yet, somehow, my boyfriend witnessed *three* separate instances of crimes in not just the area between our towns but also Fall River itself. This involved the gas station, a farmer's market, and a general store."

"And? Those sound like separate, distinct and isolated incidents," Evelyn said. I was starting to feel like I was talking to a brick wall. I turned the page of my notebook and prepared myself to reveal the most important piece of evidence.

"Are you familiar with this tattoo, Evelyn?" I asked, showing a photo in my notebook. Evelyn looked at the notebook with an impassive face, but her eyes remained stiffly on the page. The reaction was unsettling to say the least, and I felt increasingly nervous with each passing second that she stared at the photo.

"This tattoo was found—"

"Clara—" Evelyn had just been about to interrupt me, but some loud commotion on the hall interrupted both of us. Evelyn's eyes darted to her office door, and she exhaled loudly as she started massaging her temples.

"You brought him, didn't you?" she asked, sounding like a disappointed parent that was scolding a child. I stared at her, a plummeting feeling in my stomach.

The shouting in the hall grew louder and louder, and it was obvious Evelyn couldn't ignore it for much longer. She got to her feet lazily and walked calmly to the door. She opened it and walked out of her office. I followed after her, but what I saw made me freeze in my tracks right by the doorframe.

"Who the *hell* is Evelyn Reed?!" a voice roared at the top of his lungs, a shout so loud that I recoiled despite the yell having coming from Silas.

Evelyn Reed stood in the middle of the hall; her arms crossed in front of herself. Silas's eyes shook with fury as he stared right at Evelyn.

I watched with bated breath as someone walked around Silas and also looked at Evelyn with a hopeless and miserable expression.

"…Mom?" Dana asked quietly.

"See you've met my stepmom, Clara," Silas said darkly. "Right, *Eleanor Quinn*?"

20

Bang!

Silas slammed his fist on the table hard enough to feel a tinge of pain in my ears, and yet I didn't so much as flinch. So much was happening at once that I couldn't follow along with it all. Evelyn sat looking bored at the other end of a very long conference table. Dana and Silas were closer to her side of the table and were asking non-stop questions at her.

My vision was blurry, yet I tried my best to focus on Silas. He bore an outraged expression.

Dana's eyes were filled with tears, and she kept trying to reason with her mother as her voice dissolved into an incomprehensible series of shrieks.

Silas slammed his fist on the table again, but the sound didn't reach my ears this time. I felt nauseous, the bile building up in my throat was on the verge of escaping. My eyes drifted over to Silas again.

"That's enough out of you two, you're giving me a migraine," Evelyn said getting to her feet. "Sit down. This involves things you couldn't possibly understand, so don't you dare pretend that you do."

Dana plopped down onto a chair as if her body could no longer sustain the emotional weight. She buried her head into her hands and wept silently, grinding her teeth. Silas refused to sit, pacing back and forth beside the table. His hands were on the behind his head, trembling so hard I thought they might detach themselves from his wrists.

"You were going to *ruin* Clara. You would have been just fine, leaving her to rot, making sure that she'd have trouble breaking into journalism no matter where she went. Isn't that right?"

Silas brought his hands down dramatically. "And yet, that doesn't compare to the *danger* you put her through. Her and everyone in Fall River."

Evelyn rolled her eyes, massaging her forehead with her index and thumb. "Silas, you wouldn't understand—"

"Here I thought my father was only minimally involved, if at all," Silas said as he shook his head. "I never would have expected both of you to be the ones pulling the strings…You two were made for each other, you know. Both of you are *monsters*."

Dana choked another sob, one of her hands moving down to her stomach. I could tell that she felt the same—if not worse—nausea in her stomach. I was so distracted by her that I almost didn't notice Silas suddenly taking the chair next to me and facing me.

It took every ounce of my effort to face him and keep a passive expression, but my limit was almost reached. I was moments away from losing it entirely.

Trying to break eye contact with Silas was a hopeless endeavor then. I continued to stare at him silently, feeling like I was too mentally exhausted to even cry.

"Do you even know what happened to Clara's mother?" Dana asked as she looked up at Evelyn. "How could you be ok with doing this to her…to the people of Fall River…"

"The real question," Silas said without taking his eyes off of me. "Is how they thought they could get away with it—"

The door to the conference room was opened and four security guards walked in, the employee from the front desk among them. They were all on the heavier side, especially in the middle section. All of their faces were spiteful, and they seemed happy to be there. It was obvious they were looking for any excuse to rough someone up.

"Gathered up all of the security guards in the building," the front desk employee said with a sinister smile. Evelyn game him a drawn out, silent stare. "Everyone else called out today or are on their lunch break," the employee said as he shrunk back slightly.

"Right," Evelyn said, exasperated. "Clara, I believe we were interrupted. We should continue our conversation somewhere else. Besides," she paused, giving me a concerned look. "You look about ready to throw up. Let's go somewhere where you can get some fresh air."

"You're not taking her anywhere," Silas said, his voice low and steady.

"Oh ho, we're here to make sure you stay right here, boy," the employee said as the other men started smiling amongst themselves. "That's right, Silas. These gentleman will make sure you stay right here with your sister."

Silas didn't bother giving the men more than a simple glance.

"*Ten* of you couldn't keep me here." Silas's voice was the voice of someone who cannot be reasoned with. For the first time, I felt the gears in my head start turning.

"Silas, don't," I begged. The thought of him being hurt caused my heart to ache beyond my comprehension.

Silas was clearly moved by what I said. He lifted a trembling hand up to my face. I closed my eyes, letting his fingers tuck my hair behind my ear. When I opened them, there was a sea of calm in his eyes.

He gave me a reassuring look. He leaned into my ear and spoke softly.

"Go with her. I'll be there, no matter what happens. Count on it."

"Please be careful," I said as Silas sat back up on his chair.

"I'll do what I can," he answered.

A shaky smile fought against me and won; appearing on my face as I looked at Silas longingly. I couldn't form any words, so I closed the distance between us and planted a slow, drawn-out kiss on his lips. I didn't care that there were other people in the room; they faded from reality the second our lips met.

Evelyn led the way out of the conference room. I shot Dana a look and she was still leaning her head against balled up fists, though her tears had started to dry on her cheeks. Silas was still leaning against his chair comfortably.

He gave me a discrete and confident wink just as one of the four men locked the conference door behind me with a key that locked itself from the inside. I knew what thoughts were going through Silas's head.

You don't want the action to start with me in the room so that I wouldn't have to see you or anyone else getting hurt, right?

I closed my eyes and took a deep breath, hoping that whatever happened, Silas came out ok in the end.

***

"Clara," Evelyn called out to me stonily. I was standing on the steps in front of the building staring off into nothing. Evelyn waited until I acknowledged her before she faced the street again. She opened the driver's side door of a nearby car and sat inside. She turned the car on and idled, waiting for me. I opened the passenger side door and sat inside.

Evelyn didn't say a word as she drove. I sat in the passenger seat and reminisced on my rides with Caleb in his Mustang. The thought morphed into thinking of all of my friends, and I felt a warmth in my chest.

The drive lasted no more than two minutes. Our

destination was a small park that was visible from the entrance of the building. Evelyn wordlessly got out of the car and approached the park without looking back at me. I followed behind her, looking over my shoulder to see if we were being followed. The park was relatively empty, and no other cars had driven into the parking lot.

Evenly led me to a park bench near the center of the park. It was surprisingly desolate, and it wasn't hard to figure out why she chose it. Despite saying that I 'needed fresh air', I knew that there was nothing more secure than speaking where no one was around. There were no trees around either, granting her an unrestricted view of everything around us. It was a new level of privacy that not even her office, with those four closed off walls, could provide. As we were approaching the bench, I slipped one of my hands into my coat pocket as discreetly as I could. I felt the familiar click of a button and moved my hand away before Evelyn turned back around.

Once we were both seated, Evelyn waved her hand at me, as if handing me the stage. "Continue where you left off before, please," she asked. Her tone was slightly less cruel, leaning more towards that of having a vague interest.

I blinked at her a few times, wondering if she was serious. Continuing felt pointless after the confrontations made by Dana and Silas, but I realized that they never truly pieced everything together. So, I decided to continue my thoughts from before. "That tattoo that I showed you was on the arms of two people linked to criminal activity, both in the same vicinity and timeframe—"

"Go on," Evelyn urged.

"I also had a third encounter with that tattoo on someone who displayed violent tendencies, and yet was trying his best to control them so that he may integrate himself with society—"

"Move on."

"That makes three individuals with tattoos, something that is common in gangs and gang-related activities. These three individuals—"

"Please, continue," she said, growing impatient.

I swallowed hard. "The timing of these encounters was suspicious due to the mayor of this city, Arden Bay, having announced a sharp decrease in inmates. The exact methods of how this decrease were never shared nor stated in your feature. This led me to believe—"

"Believe what, exactly? Tell me."

"I suspect that Arden Bay, in an attempt to make the city's statistics look better, released prisoners from its prisons and immediately moved them outside of the city's limits. They then boasted about a lower prison population and a successful decarceration effort, even though they just moved the problem somewhere else."

Evelyn looked at me without saying anything. I took the opportunity to continue with my point, my eyes unwaveringly staring at hers.

"Not only did the move the problem somewhere else, but they moved the prisoners to a nearby smaller town, Fall River, since it wouldn't have strong representation in the state legislature to fight back. Arden Bay believed that it would get away with it."

I clenched my fist. "Fall River experienced a kidnapping, several separate instances of crime, but it all came to a head when numerous stores were subjected to armed robberies. It was during this large-scale robbery that my own mother was sent to the hospital, where she is still intubated."

Evelyn's eyes did not soften in the slightest. "What do the tattoos have anything to do with anything?" she asked, trying to poke holes in my analysis.

"If you removed certain members of the same gang, you increase the risk that they'll talk if they get arrested in other towns and jurisdictions. If you release the entire gang, then you lower the possibility of them talking about Arden Bay in a negative light since they let everyone in your gang go at once."

Evelyn continued her emotionless glare for a long time. Eventually, she faltered, and an impressed look appeared on her face.

"That is quite the detective work you've done," she told me, serious. "It's commendable."

Her words didn't make me feel any relief in the slightest. I looked at her, feeling deeply unsettled. Her refusal to acknowledge the condition of my mother caused my heartbeat to quicken in anger, and it took all of my effort not to snap at her.

"Are you…confirming that it's the truth?"

Evelyn leaned back on the bench and pulled out a cigarette. She lit it and took a long drag, going out of her way to release the smoke just near enough to my face so that I could get a good whiff of the smell.

"You went digging into something you shouldn't have, Clara," Evenly said, placing extra emphasis on the last word. "This is a matter of the city of Arden Bay and the town of Fall River."

I widened my eyes at her, shocked. Before I had any chance to say anything at all, Evelyn suddenly leaned in close to me and started talking with a quiet, albeit threatening voice.

"This is what you are going to do, Clara. You are going to go right back to Fall River, and you are going to accept that your town's local paper is not going to hire you for a full-time position. You are going to give up on working in journalism, forever. You will accept that you were all wrong about this, and you won't mention this to anyone."

"Why do you think I'm not worried about admitting this to you? You do know what would happen if you even tried to bring this to light, right?" she asked, a tone of warning in her voice. "This involves not just the Mayor, but also the Police Chief, City Council members, and countless others. I was fed this story by a high-ranking city official. You'd be messing with deep ties; ties you do not want to mess with."

Evelyn's eyes were sharp as daggers, and I couldn't help but flinch multiple times as she almost spat into my face. Once she was done, she pulled back and leaned on the chair again.

"You—you're saying you were fed this story?" I asked, my voice coming out much weaker than I intended. Evelyn didn't look at me as she responded.

"You think reporters uncover things at this level? I'm embedded with City Hall. I have direct lines to the Mayor's office, the Police Chief's PR team, and even individual police officers. It's an entire network, and I'm told what to report, always."

I blinked multiple times at her in disbelief. I couldn't wrap my head around what she was saying. "You're saying you report what you're told? Even if it's wrong? Why? Why would you do that?"

Evelyn looked at me like I had suddenly started talking to her in a different language. "Exclusive access, promotions, endless benefits, my own office…you ever heard of career advancement?" She took another long drag of the cigarette, this time releasing the smoke of it straight up into the air.

I clenched both of my fists tight. "I always believed journalism to be about spreading the truth, and to be united with my community. I never thought it was about spreading lies to just advance my career."

With a quick, practiced motion, Evelyn jabbed the cigarette into the bench beneath us with a frustrated twist. "That's why, Clara, you were never meant to be a reporter. You would never last in the world of journalism. So, give. It. Up."

"This was never meant to be directed towards you, Clara," she confided. "You simply flew too close to the sun; your story touching too much of the truth. Trust me, I'd have wished for anyone else to have written that feature but you."

"And about your mother? My suggestion? Be happy that she survived and move on. If the crime worries you, suggest moving to another town."

...Monster...you absolute monster...

I swallowed my unnerving anger that rose up from the depths of my heart. "And what of Silas's father?"

Evelyn's eyes jerked to the side at the mention of him, but she quickly recovered. "I married Silas's father out convenience—no, necessity. Gerald Quinn once told me that if you can control the data, you control reality. Social calendar, image, everything. If he thought destroying a thousand lives would ensure he got his way," Evelyn's eyes momentarily flickered with fear. "...Then he wouldn't hesitate. He'd call it an *acceptable cost*. That was when I knew that he was the man that would culminate my ambitions to reality."

I got to my feet, fighting the severe sense of lightheadedness that I felt. I hesitated on walking away, and Evelyn took the opportunity to tell me of one last parting threat.

"Remember what I said about ties, Clara. One phone call is all it would take to have the entire city of Arden Bay on you. Trespassing, breaking and entering, disorderly conduct...it doesn't matter what reason I give them. I could have you taken into custody for a long, long, time. So, I would suggest keeping this conversation between us."

I turned my back to Evelyn and tried my best to walk away as composed as possible. Truth was that her threats were more than frightening. The worst thing about it was that it didn't just apply to me, either. After all, Lauren was the photographer and also involved in the feature. If I wasn't careful, then she might get caught in this, too.

Unfortunately, I couldn't fake my composure for long. The moment I turned and started walking away from her, my bag slipped to the ground, along with the small microcassette recorder I snuck into my pocket while approaching the park bench. I felt a sinking sensation throughout my entire body as I saw it land just beside my feet, clearly within Evelyn's sight.

I bent down and picked the recorder and my bag as quickly as I could, and against my better judgement I snuck a passing glance back at Evelyn to see if she caught sight of the recorder.

Evelyn's eyes were wide. Her pupils were small and looked like slits as they shook with barely contained fury. Her entire body was stock still, as if she was processing her next series of moves all in her head.

Before I could think anything of it, I set off on a desperate run towards the parking lot.

Please, Silas…

I prayed and begged that somehow, even as improbable as it looked like considering he was locked in that room with four grown men—

You said I could count on you. Please…

I set my eyes on the parking lot and immediately felt my heart skip a beat as I saw Silas drive in on his motorcycle, his helmet already on his head. There was no time for him to put on my helmet; I hopped on the bike quickly with experience.

"Get me to the nearest phone, now!" I yelled as loud as I could over the roaring engine. Silas set the bike in motion without any hesitation.

21

Silas sought out the nearest public payphone and idled in front of it. I kicked off the bike and pulled out a quarter, slamming it into the coin slot. I knew I could afford the time. Evelyn wouldn't risk calling in a high-level police operation from the side of the road; she needed to reach a secured landline to give any orders.

I pulled out my notebook from my bag as quickly as I could and entered the phone number to Lauren's grandparents' house. I had made sure to get it from Lauren before leaving Fall River. "Lauren! I'm so glad you picked up," I shrieked. Hearing her voice on the other side of the line almost made me break down in tears.

"Lauren, listen to this," I paused, lifting up my recorder and playing it for a few seconds. Evelyn's voice crackled from the recorder and sounded just as icily through the recording than in real life, if not more so. I waited until Lauren listened to enough of it to get the idea. "You heard that?"

"Clara, you were right…" Lauren trailed off. "Lauren, please tell the others. And do not go home, they might look for you there."

"What happens now, Clara?" she asked. I could tell from her shaking voice just how nervous she truly was. "We bring the truth to light, Lauren. That's the only thing I can do now." I gripped the phone tighter. "For my mom."

"You're going to come back here, aren't you?"

"We need to get out of Arden Bay as quickly as we can. I'm not sure where we're going to go, but going back to town is our safest bet."

"Got it," is all Lauren said before hanging up the phone. Knowing her, she was going to do the impossible to make sure everyone knew about this. I tried placing the phone back onto the hook, but the sudden sound behind me caused me to drop the phone as it hung loosely by its cord.

Silas had set his kickstand down and had gotten off the bike while I was on the phone. Just as I was going to hang the phone, he collapsed on the ground just by my feet.

"Silas!"

I got down and carefully removed his helmet, careful not to otherwise move his body. I gasped when I saw the condition of his face, the helmet nearly falling out of my grasp.

Silas'ss jaw contained several purplish bruises, the dark color turning into shades of yellow and green. His cheekbone was swollen, pulled taut with inflammation. There was a thin cut on his eyebrow that had dried blood flaking away, and a deep gash on his lip that was starting to scab. There was a stray trickle of blood that dried a path down the side of his cheek, one that originated from the very top of his head.

I started to truly analyze the rest of Silas's body. He had bruises all over himself, and he was clearly lying on one side of his back to avoid having to put pressure on the other side. My eyes widened when I noticed that unlike his previous fights, this time both of Silas's knuckles were bloody and damaged.

I covered my mouth with both of my hands, staring at his right hand; the hand that Silas uses to pitch. Silas followed my line of sight and lifted his hand dismissively.

"There's no point…taking care of this hand. Not when…you're in need of help," he struggled to say. I watched, horrified, as Silas grimaced as he started to get to his feet.

Knowing there'd be no point stopping him, I stood beside him and offered him my hand. Silas took it without a second thought. "Thanks for taking my helmet off, I needed to take a quick breather now that I knew that you were safe," he said like nothing else mattered in the world.

I wiped the tears building up in my eyes, knowing there was an important job we had to do.

"Silas…Can you get me to Fall River?"

Silas bent over at the waist, something that I knew took him tremendous effort to do. He brought his lips against mine softly, and I closed the small gap between them eagerly.

"Even if it kills me," Silas answered. "Before anything else, though, give me that phone number you used to call Lauren. I ripped out the page from my notebook and handed it to him, which he stashed deep in his pocket."

After putting his helmet back on, Silas took his time putting my helmet on my head, taking extra care to secure it properly. He lifted his visor to be able to see me eye-to-eye.

"You're going to need to hold on tighter than ever before, you understand?"

I nodded, feeling my anxiety building in ways I had never felt before.

Despite the situation and the sudden emergence of the far-off sound of police sirens, I couldn't help but yearn for Silas. I wanted him to hold me, to tell me that everything was going to be fine.

And yet, you couldn't do that right then, could you? You couldn't assure me that everything would be fine, not this time.

Just like the first time I rode with him, Silas looked at me through the rearview mirror, waiting for a sign that I was ready. The sounds of the police sirens grew louder still, as they at last turned the corner and came into view.

I took a deep breath, preparing myself for whatever came next.

I'm coming back home, mom.

The second he felt my squeeze his sides, Silas took off flying. We were a blur of movement, the bike flying at a speed I had never before experienced. The police cruisers sped up behind us, giving chase and refusing to let us out of their sight.

***

It couldn't be clearer that Silas had a deep understanding of Arden Bay's intricate roads. Silas navigated the city's narrow streets, side alleys, and congested traffic with ease. The sounds of traffic, the sound of the motorcycle's engine, and most of all the wail of police sirens filled my ears.

I realized that Silas was taking advantage of being on a motorcycle to evade the officers. The police cruisers were in boxy, powerful sedans. Due to their size, they were forced to be more cautious on tight turns and sudden stops.

Because of this, Silas continually opted for backstreet alleys where their cars wouldn't dare fit into. I was consistently surprised at Silas's confidence and fearless maneuvering. Not once did he end up in a dead-end, and he was never cornered. It was the expertise one demonstrates after living in the city for years. We hadn't agreed on a destination before we set off, so I trusted he had a destination in mind. It was pointless trying to have a conversation while in movement, regardless.

I felt my stomach drop as I saw Silas turn into a wide street, one that was entirely blocked off at the end by police cruisers. It was a sea of red and blue lights, and there was clearly no way around them. Going back the way we came wasn't an option either, as we had another cruiser following behind us. The other issue was that our speed was too high to safely come to a stop. By the time Silas slammed on the brakes, we'd be much too close to the officers ahead of us.

What do we do, Silas?

Silas leaned the bike over, and the world tilted sideways. I felt the sudden, unnatural drag as the back tire began to complain, a dry, grinding screech that made the hair on my arms stand up. I tightened my arms around his waist, instinctively pressing myself closer to his back. I could feel Silas's muscles tensing under my hands, the world momentarily reduced to the sound of sliding rubber. Then, just as suddenly as it began, the bike snapped upright and settled into a perfect silence, leaving my heart pounding in my chest and the smell of hot asphalt in the air.

The front of the bike was now facing sideways instead of straight towards the cruisers blocking off the street. Silas had performed a deliberate slide to come to a perfect stop. He took a quick look at me in the rearview mirror before taking off again, this time straight into another alley.

The chase lasted for well over ten minutes. Silas consistently evaded the cruisers, and yet there were a few scares. I could tell that he was starting to get worn down, and I knew it was because of me. He was afraid of going too fast, of taking turns that were too dangerous, in order to avoid me getting hurt. I had a feeling that if he had been chased on his own, Silas would have already lost the police. But I was holding him back, a figurative anchor in his escape.

At last, Silas brought the bike to an idle in an obscure alley between two large apartment buildings. "Clara!" he yelled. I jerked to attention, his voice sounding alien to me after the events of the chase. "Yes!" I answered.

"I'm going to take you to a bus stop. The bus will take you straight to Fall River. There's only one stop since Fall River is such a small town. Got it?!"

I nodded as I heard the information. "Wait, are you suggesting we split up—" I couldn't finish my question. Silas set the bike in motion again. The bus stop was immediately in view, and luckily the next bus was about to depart. I knew I had to move quickly, so I got off the bike as soon as Silas stopped.

Silas removed his bookbag and handed it to me in order to avoid wasting time. "Listen to me, I'm going to ride to Fall River the long way around. I'm going to try to meet you at that stop. Clara, lay low until you get there," he instructed as he removed the helmet from my head.

I opened my mouth to say something, but Silas lurched forward and was gone in the blink of an eye. I heard sirens quickly approaching, so I started moving as fast as I could. I ran to a nearby trash can and left my helmet on the ground beside it. This pained me, as he had bought it with me in mind. Taking it with me wasn't an option, however. It was too bulky for me to carry during my escape. I then approached the bus.

I opened Silas's bag and fished out his wallet. I pulled out the cash needed to board the bus and got on, heading straight to the back row. There was already someone in the very last row, so I sat two rows ahead of him. The man barely acknowledged me, focusing on the view beside the window.

Just as I was about to sit down, I saw a rush of police cruisers fly right past the bus. I put a hand over my heart, trying to calm it. The only thing in my mind was Silas. The thing I feared more than his capture was him getting in an accident, one that would injure him or even worse, take his life.

I looked at Silas's bag, hoping it could distract me. Tears started to fall freely from my eyes as I slowly pulled out the same laminated photo of myself that I had found just the night before. That night—that dearly special night—felt like it had happened more than a lifetime ago. I turned the photo around, and I nearly felt my heart stop when I noticed and read the words that had been written behind it.

Clara Monroe, 11. The girl I've loved since the very first time I laid my eyes on her.

I pulled the photo towards my chest, straight over my heart. I did my best to stifle my sobs, but it was a pointless endeavor.

22

The bus was about twenty minutes from Fall River when it came to an abrupt stop. I had thought it was safe now that we had left Arden Bay's city limits, but clearly, I couldn't be more wrong. When I looked out the window, I saw the bus was stopped by a police cruiser that said Fall River on the side.

A roadblock by Fall River police?

The officer asked to board the bus, and the driver complied as he opened the door for them. I started to panic, looking all around for somewhere I could possibly hide. I racked my brain as much as I could, but it looked hopeless. I was cornered, and there wasn't anywhere I could go.

When I looked behind me, I made eye contact with the man on the last row. He gestured for me to come over to him, pointing at the window seat to his left. Without any hesitation, I walked over to him just as the officer started to go up the steps of the bus.

I threw my bags onto the corner and ducked down into the space of the last seats so that I'd be out of direct view. The man then boxed me in, making it seem like there wasn't anyone beside him.

For a reason he didn't explain, the man opened the bottle of soda in his hand and took a long swig. He then leaned back onto his seat and rolled his head back as far as he could onto the headrest, feigning being asleep. With a subtle gesture, the man offered the soda bottle to me. I grabbed it and hid it amongst my other things.

I heard the officers' steps walk down the aisle. He was moving slowly and deliberately, clearly making sure to check every individual seat. He had no doubt been given my description and had been instructed to bring anyone in that even remotely matched it.

He was coming close to the back of the bus, and I felt my skin crawl.

"Anyone beside you, sir?" the officer asked just overhead. His voice was *so close*. I instinctively covered my mouth with a trembling hand, trying to cover up my breathing. Luckily, the chairs were covered at the bottom so he couldn't see me beneath the seat. He had to look over the man sitting next to me so see me.

The man didn't answer, so the officer took a few steps to get closer. I closed my eyes, starting to accept that it was over.

Suddenly, I heard a repulsive sound just above me. My head jerked up to see what had just happened. The man had been storing the soda in his mouth this entire time. He waited until the officer got close to fake vomit all over his own shirt, making disgusting sounds and gargling noises. He also coughed, selling the idea that he was alive, and most likely just drunk. The soda had taken a gross orange color, looking even closer to vomit than anything else.

I heard the officer back away, revolted. Without another word, his footsteps went back down the aisle. He exchanged a quick word with the bus driver and walked right off. The man with vomit on his shirt continued to keep his eyes closed, pretending to be asleep. It wasn't until the bus driver closed the doors and put the pus in motion that the man moved aside to give me space to get back up.

"Th—thank you," I stammered. I couldn't believe a stranger was so willing to help me, especially with evading the police of all things. "Why did you help me?"

"Something about you made me want to help you young lady. Besides," the man said, giving me a short wink. "We all have a little run-in with the law sometimes."

I returned to my seat two rows in front of the back row and nodded at him in appreciation again. He returned it, looking funny with his shirt tinged orange.

***

As I suspected, the police didn't bother investigating the bus for a second time after the initial inspection. There weren't any other interruptions to the bus as it drove the rest of the 20 minutes towards the familiar sights of Fall River.

The bus driver brought the bus to a crawl. I got to my feet and gathered my things. Before moving into the aisle, I looked to the back to say farewell to the man that helped me. I smiled quietly, seeing that the man was deep asleep for real this time. I made my way to the front, thanking the driver as I disembarked. I saw a thought cloud the driver's face as he saw me, but he didn't say anything as he closed the door behind me.

I stood at the bus stop for a lingering moment. I was alone, and I didn't know what to do first. I imagined that Silas would somehow already be here. For a moment, I thought of the worst. But I shook my head to get rid of the idea. He mentioned that it was a longer way around. Even if he was moving faster than the bus was, it's understandable if he took longer to get here.

I was about to take my first step when I heard it; the sound that made the entire world around me start to crumble.

Five police cruisers, their sirens suddenly started blaring as they came into view, turned the corner and quickly closed in towards me. I flinched, unsure of whether to start running or to just give up.

The cars fanned out, cutting out any possibilities of escape.

No, this can't be the end.

I turned around and took off running, my feet hitting the ground as fast as they'd ever carried me. I heard the sirens closing in on me from behind, inching closer and closer by the second—

Just then, a car drifted into view from directly in front of me. The car quickly accelerated, blasting his horn. I came to an abrupt stop, my eyes widening as two, three, no, four cars followed closely behind the first car.

The car in the lead drove right past me and I saw who was inside the driver's seat for the first time.

Ralph's face, serious with determination and yet sporting a grin that spanned ear to ear, looked back at me. Ralph tugged on the steering wheel, causing it to drift and cut off the quickly approaching police cruisers. The other cars closed in and similarly started surrounding me from all directions. I looked around in a daze, unsure what I was meant to do.

"Clara!"

Caleb's voice managed to cut through all of the roaring engines. His white mustang was heading straight for me. Caleb drifted the car and brough the car to a stop right in front of me, the tires screeching loudly. I took a preemptive step backward, yet it wasn't necessary. Caleb had measured the distance perfectly, and he brought it to a stop just a few feet in front of me. He leaned towards the open passenger window before shouting:

"In, now, Clara!"

I pulled on the passenger-side door handle and threw my things inside. I tucked my legs in and before I had a chance to close the door, Caleb launched the car forward. The Mustang's engine groaned with an unrivaled ferocity I'd never heard before.

I reached out to put on my seatbelt, my brain a hazy mess as I was jolted from side to side as Caleb took off. I looked behind us as the other cars that were drifting around us all dispersed in different directions.

"All of those cars were a distraction? Who was that—"

"You were right about them coming to look for Lauren at her house, Clara," Caleb spat. His eyes laser focused on the road. I was stunned to silence. "Her parents called her grandparents' house and told her that two officers did come looking for her. They pretended they didn't know where she was."

I felt my stomach drop. "Lauren…Is she safe?" I managed to ask as I was being moved around in the seat.

"She's at the drop-off point—She's safe!"

Caleb pulled the steering wheel and moved the lever next to himself, making intricate changes to the stick shift. The Mustang obeyed his commands, making a tight turn with ease as the car drifted before Caleb accelerated forwards again.

"Caleb—" my voice was tight, a mix of adrenaline and surprise. I felt a sudden wave of emotions.

"Caleb I'm so sorry for everything…"

I watched as Caleb tightened his grip on the steering wheel. Everything I had meant to tell him had started to escape me all at once.

"I shouldn't have hurt you the way that I did…you didn't deserve that. Caleb, I'm sorry…!

Caleb adjusted his rearview mirror. Yet I didn't need to look behind us to know the truth: there was a police cruiser behind us. The distraction with the other cars seemed to work since there was only one cruiser on us, but it didn't leave us in the clear. That meant that the chase still wasn't over.

"Forget the past, Clara," Caleb paused, shaking his head. "You're trying to save this town. I'm going to do what it takes to make sure that happens."

I felt myself press against the seat. Caleb was accelerating, pushing the Mustang even further. Caleb took another sharp turn, the rear wheel snagged against the sidewalk, jolting the entire car upwards. Caleb handled it with expertise, refusing to lose control of the car.

"It's not just about your mom…It could have been my mom, or Ralph's, or Lauren's. It's only a matter of time."

I reached out and placed one of my hands onto Caleb's extended arms.

"Caleb—"

"We're putting an end to this, *now!*" Caleb roared. "Just know that I'm going to make sure nothing happens to you. I'm not doing this just for you, Clara. I'm doing this for my family, for Fall River, for *everyone*. I'm going to make sure that no one lays a single finger on you until you deliver that tape—"

I figured that Caleb was headed towards the farmer's market parking lot. The lot was in view, and with just another two minutes of driving we would have made it. Caleb's latest maneuver also let him lose the officer chasing from behind.

It was right then that another cruiser, waiting on

standby, caught sight of us. Caleb didn't have time to react before the cruiser inched forwards and effortlessly pit maneuvered Caleb's Mustang. We spiraled out of control, ramming into a nearby tree. The entire world went dark.

****

I opened my eyes, trying to force my eyes to focus. The world wouldn't stop spinning. I felt my body in motion, yet I was clearly waking up from being unconscious. Memories of the crash started coming back to me little by little.

The Mustang slammed against the tree from the rear end of the car from the driver's side. I winced, immediately thinking about Caleb's condition, hoping that he was okay.

My hearing was starting to return to me, which is when I realized for the first time that I couldn't hear anything until then. As my hearing came back, I realized something was yelling at me from just above me.

The world began to come back into focus, and I saw Caleb's strained face just above mine. I blinked up at him, alarmed, as my spatial awareness started to kick back in. Caleb was princess carrying me, and it was obvious that he was just one tick about delirious. He wasn't walking straight, and he was blinking profusely, trying to focus on everything around him.

"…Clara…you…you…awake?"

"…Yes, I'm awake, Caleb," I struggled to say.

I heard several voices yelling from behind us, and I could tell that they were quickly gaining on us. I squirmed in Caleb's arms, taking in our surroundings. Caleb had collected me from the Mustang and took off for the woods. This made it so the officers had to follow us on foot, giving us a slight advantage.

"Clara, can you run?" Caleb asked. He sounded about ready to pass out right then and there. I noticed just then the blood trickling down from the side of his head. I felt like hyperventilating knowing that Caleb might have been suffering from a medical emergency and yet he was focusing all of his energy on helping me escape.

"Yes, Caleb. Please, let them take you to the hospital—"

Caleb didn't wait another second. He placed my feet on the ground and yelled at the top of his lungs:

"Clara—got to the lot!"

I watched as Caleb ran full speed in another direction, catching the attention of the officers. I bit down on my lip as I faced the lot again and took off, making sure not to waste the opportunity Caleb was working so desperately hard to create for me to guarantee my escape.

23

Keep running.

My vision was blurry from the tears that wouldn't stop filling my eyes.

Just keep running, Clara.

I tightened my grip on my bag. Caleb must have grabbed it from the car wreckage.

Don't let it all be for nothing.

I knew that Caleb would want me to get away, no matter what. I knew he would want me to keep running. To go, go, go.

I sobbed loudly as my emotions boiled over, my breathing grew uncontrolled. All I could think about was the sight of Caleb just before he was willing to sacrifice everything for me. I thought of the words he had shared with me in the car, as he had shared his deepest feelings right in the open, and yet I didn't get the chance to share any of my own.

I felt myself gain a second wind, my legs pushing me forwards as the farmer's market lot grew closer.

"Clara!" a familiar voice called out. A few cars were gathered in a circle in the center of the lot. I approached the circle, seeing Mason, Lauren, and Emmy were among those around. They waited for me to arrive, clearly waiting for me to tell them what to do next.

I worked out that their plan thus far was for Caleb to bring me to this rendezvous point. However, what we did now depended on me.

I thought about it as I ran up so that I would know exactly what to say when I got there.

"Take me here, please!" I begged as I desperately reached into my bag for the business card Audrey Price gave me.

Huh?

I looked and looked, but the business card was nowhere in sight. It must have dropped from my bag at some point during the chase.

"I lost the address…but I know where it is. It's near the local paper!"

Mason nodded at me in understanding.

"I'll make some calls to tell everyone to head there," one of the guys in the circle said.

"No! That'll just be easier for the police to follow and find it, right?" Emmy warned.

"That's right, I think we should split up the cars again to create as much confusion as possible," Lauren added.

"We need to get moving," Mason said as he looked

in the direction I came from. More police cars were approaching, sirens blaring.

"Ralph told us all about the recording you have," one of the nearby guys said. "Make sure all of this isn't for nothing. Don't give that tape up."

"Come on, let's go," Mason hurried as he opened the rear door for me. Mason, Lauren, Emmy and I got into Mason's car as he turned on the car. The other two cars in the lot did the same, and all three vehicles drove off in different directions. The other two drivers, knowing our destination, took additional precautions to head as far away from it as possible.

"Who—who were all of those guys?" I asked, trying my best to distract myself.

"Guys from Fall River's baseball team," Lauren answered from the front passenger seat.

"Once they heard about your voice recording and that Lauren listened to it herself, they all volunteered their cars to be distractions." Emmy smiled. "Not everyone agreed to help, but those closest to Ralph did. He told them about his mother and what happened to your mom…they decided to help after that."

"Ralph can be very convincing," Mason said distractedly over his shoulder.

Suddenly, Lauren turned around and looked at me from the seat in front of me.

"Clara, take off those pants," she deadpanned.

I blinked at her. "Come again?"

"Emmy, switch with me. I need to move to the back seat," Lauren said as she made her way to the back. "Got it."

As soon as Emmy and Lauren switched places, Lauren started to lift up her shirt. She paused just before she lifted it above her head.

"Eyes forward, mister," Lauren said quietly as she looked at Mason through the rearview mirror. I thought I caught their eyes meeting through the reflection, which could only happen if Mason was checking her out in the first place.

"Right, right," Mason said sheepishly.

"Clara, you need to swap clothes with me," Lauren said. "You and I have the same color hair. The cops have your description. So, if I'm wearing your clothes, then they'll chase after me instead of you."

I was taken aback by her plan. It was risky, but it just might work if the officer saw us both in passing.

"Let's do it," I said, starting to take my jacket off.

Now in Lauren's clothes, I settled into the seat. Mason drove an unassuming sedan, which was perfect for fitting in with regular traffic, but was definitely not the best for speeding away from the police. Thankfully, it seemed that the cruisers that arrived had chosen the other cars to chase down.

I clasped my hands in front of me. I made a silent prayer that my gamble would pay off. It was my only chance, and if it failed then there was nothing else I could do.

***

We reached the front of Audrey Prices' small business without much excitement. "Everyone get out,

I'm going to park the car far away and walk over so it's less suspicious," Mason instructed.

"I'll stay with him, you two go," Lauren said.

Emmy and I got out of the car, and I saw Lauren start to make her way up to the front seat again. Once we walked up to the storefront, I desperately started to rap on the glass door. The door was frosted, so I couldn't exactly see inside. It was clear that the lights were off, though, and it looked like no one was inside. Even still, I was counting that she was in the back somewhere.

"Come on," I said as I knocked on the door harder and harder. "What are we going to do, Clara?" Emmy asked, getting worried.

I was about to knock on the door again when I heard the shrill sound of a police cruiser raising its alarm. I turned slowly as the police officer remained in his car and looked at us through his passenger side door. His eyes looked me up and down, taking in my appearance. He was about to speak onto his radio when something caught his attention in front of him.

I followed his gaze to see Mason and Lauren in the middle of the road, acting like they were caught red-handed. They took off running, and the officer drove after them. I took a calming breath, remembering that Lauren and I had swapped clothes. Clearly, her plan had worked.

Growing desperate, I turned around to knock on the door harder when I saw Audrey staring at me from the sidewalk.

"Clara…?"

"Audrey!" I broke down, starting to sob right in front of her eyes. Her face took on a sense of alarm, and she quickly walked up to her office door and unlocked it. "Inside, now," she said.

"Clara, does Silas know where this office is?" Emmy asked. I thought for a moment and realized Silas wouldn't have any way of knowing where Audrey's business was. "No, he doesn't," I answered.

"Lock it behind you, I'm going to the local paper, then. Silas might go there looking for you. If he does, then I'll tell him to come here." Odds were that Silas would go to the local paper thinking I would want to publish the story that way, so I agreed to her plan. Audrey nodded as well and locked up. Despite the windows all being frosted, she closed all of the curtains and sat me down on a chair.

"I—I have a story," I managed. I steeled myself, fully knowing that this wasn't over until the story was told. "I can't count on local paper following through with it, like you said. I thought of you, Audrey."

Audrey gave me a ravenous look. "You know I love a good story. You did the right thing, Clara. Let's print it."

I blinked at her a few times. "This is really bad, Audrey. Are you sure you don't want to hear about it before—"

"I don't care what it is," she cut me off. "You've got police from all over town looking for you, Clara. We're printing it."

I nodded at her resolutely. I couldn't be happier to have someone like her on my side. Even if she was in it for notoriety, or career advancement, like Evelyn said. She was desperate to publish the *truth*. And for that, I couldn't be more grateful.

Audrey and I began to work like a machine. I wordlessly provided all of the evidence to her, making notes on what I had learned since I never got the opportunity to do so as I discovered it. During the process, I played the recorder for Audrey to hear. She had a winded look on her face, as if she was in disbelief of what she was hearing.

As Evelyn's recorded voice filled the empty space, my eyes drifted down to the table we are working on. Papers, pens, and monitors were scattered around the humble office. I imagined working here, alongside Audrey. The thought excited me more than it did compared to imagining working in the intimidating office of The Town Local. I started playing with another microcassette tape that was left over on the desk when I started to hear something that sounded like muted voices arguing just outside the office. I walked over to pause the recorder Audrey was holding and listened closely to the voices.

Is that…Dana?

My stomach plummeted. While Audrey looked at the door, puzzled, I looked around frantically for a hiding spot for the tape. After no time at all, I heard the loud shattering of the glass door.

I turned, shocked, to see a manic-looking Evelyn Reed standing on the other side of the shattered entrance. Her eyes seemed to devour the sight of me whole. Her hands tightened over the crowbar in her hands.

"You…have…no…idea…" she emphasized every word. "What you have done."

Audrey remained stock still, knowing just as well as I did that Evelyn was capable of doing anything. She stepped over the broken glass, her kitten heels cracking the glass beneath it.

"You thought you could get away with this? That I would simply let you ruin everything I worked so hard to build?"

"Mom, please, stop this!"

I looked behind Evelyn and saw Dana sitting in the back of a car, her voice sounding desperate. Evelyn shot her a look that shut Dana up. Evelyn approached slowly, her knuckles white as she gripped the crowbar even tighter.

"How did you know she'd come here?" Audrey asked, her voice faltering. I shot her a look, realizing she was doing anything just to buy some more time.

With a smooth and practiced motion, Evelyn slid out a business card and tossed it towards us. The card landed on the ground just beneath me. I didn't need to look at it to know; it was the very card that I had dropped. That meant that it fell in front of the park bench.

I felt my stomach go into knots.

Is it…over?

"The tape, now—"

I felt a pang in my heart as I saw the shadow of someone else entering the store behind Evelyn. He walked around her and swiftly removed the crowbar from her hands.

"That's enough of that, mom."

Silas threw the crowbar effortlessly to the other side of the office. It fell to the ground with a loud pang. Evelyn stared at it longingly as Silas walked past her and approached me. He didn't stop until there were mere inches between our faces.

"Caught up to you," he murmured.

"About time," I whispered.

"Silas," Evelyn's voice was erratic and unstable. "Do you know what your father and I have sacrificed for you and your sister? You have no idea everything your father has done—"

"You're right about that, I don't know exactly what he's done," Silas cut her off. He never once took his eyes off of me while he spoke. "That's exactly the problem. I don't know the depths you two have gone. I probably won't ever scratch the surface of it all."

Silas started to smile at me when we both heard another series of footsteps cross into the store. I felt the hair on my arms stand up in alarm as I heard the sound of broken glass being crushed by two large shoes. The footsteps approached, and I saw Silas's eyes widened in fear even before we heard the voice.

"Turn around and face me, Silas."

Silas didn't move for a long time. I willed him to continue looking at me, to stop him from turning away. Yet I could see that he was no longer finding any solace in my eyes. He bore a hopeless expression, weariness seeping into every inch of his face.

"Hey…dad," Silas choked out.

Silas turned around to face his father, and I looked around him to see the man that took Silas away from me four years ago.

Silas's father ran a hand through his hair, the slicked-back style now disheveled, making him look less corporate and more like a predator who was getting ready to go hunting. He wore slim-fitting pants with an impressive belt. His dress shirt wasn't paired with a suit, but what's left is more vulnerable and menacing. The silk button-down shirt was untucked, and he started to roll up his sleeves up to his elbows, revealing muscular forearms. The shirt was perfect, the kind of material that somehow never crumbles.

He turned his head and his gaze caught mine. Theres a cold fire in them, a ruthless and calculating ambition that terrified me to the core. It was the eyes of a man that has managed to accomplish absolutely everything he'd set out to accomplish in life and didn't acknowledge failure in the slightest.

"You're here, Gerald," Evelyn spoke lightly. As if a switch had been flipped, Evelyn had suddenly abandoned the manic look in her eyes and was now acting reserved and professional.

As if that could cover up the fact that she broke down the glass door with a crowbar...

"Gerald...I am so sorry about—"

"We'll talk about this another time, *dear*," Silas's father said with an eerie edge to this voice. "I'm here to bring an end to this," he said, addressing Silas again.

"Bring me the tape, Silas."

24

"…You followed me," Silas swallowed. "How?"

"You think I bought you that motorcycle out of the kindness of my heart, Silas?" Gerald took a step forward, sliding his hands into his pockets comfortably. "I installed a vehicle tracker on that bike. If you ever decided to run away from home, I wanted to make sure I'd be able to track you down."

Silas gave a raspy, humorless laugh. "One of the few things I was happy you gave me, and even that had a hidden motive behind it."

Gerald looked taken aback. "One of the few things, Silas? Do you hear yourself?"

He took a long step forward, closing the distance between him and Silas little by little. As he inched closer, he seemed to loom over us; his form taking on a darker and more sinister appearance.

"I've done everything for you, Silas. All of this has

been for you. I saw potential in you for baseball as a child, so I laid the groundwork for you to make it to the professional level. I already have a contract already made so that you could join Arden Bay's team. It's thanks to the connections and money I've made that made something like that possible."

Gerald lifted a thumb and pointed it behind himself, towards Evelyn. "Your mother and I have built an empire of connections in Arden Bay. Ties that you and your sister will be able to take advantage of when you're older."

"You mean to tell me that money and power wasn't what you two were after?" Silas shook his head slowly. "You don't care about us. You only care about yourselves."

Gerald took another step forward. His voice dropped, losing all pretense of paternal care. "We built this empire so you wouldn't have to struggle, Silas. Power is protection. And right now, we're securing the final piece of that protection. A deal that will make the Quinn name unbreakable for generations.

He gestured dismissively toward the town outside. "To get the state funding we need, a $2 billion infrastructure grant, Arden Bay must be statistically flawless. The best in the state. No crime, perfect outcomes." Gerald gave a cold, humorless smile. "The measures your mother and I took were necessary to ensure that data was pristine."

"Your pitching career wasn't just a game, Silas. It was the face of that flawless image. You were the golden prodigy from the perfect town, the guaranteed success story that validated our entire operation. You were the proof of the Quinn legacy." Gerald's eyes narrowed with disappointment.

"And you risked that entire dynasty for a *girl*."

Gerald took another step forward. "Are you going to give up this opportunity that I'm giving you, Silas? Fame and Arden Bay's pro team are within your grasp. Will you let that go?"

For the first time, I flinched as I took a slight step backwards. I looked at Silas's back and wondered for a second what his response was going to be. He'd been in love with baseball for as long as I could remember. This could be the opportunity of a lifetime for him, and should he refuse, he might not make it to the same level of fame and wealth.

Would he be tempted…to take his offer?

"You look terrible, Silas," Gerald sighed suddenly.

I nervously raised my head, which had started to drift down to the ground, to face Silas and acknowledged his condition for the first time. I was so happy to see him that I hadn't noticed how he looked worse than the last time I had seen him. Silas was almost incapable of standing on his own two feet, clearly having to deliberately maintain his balance or risk falling over. He took long, deliberate breaths, and I could almost hear him wheezing slightly from behind him. He was placing most of his weight on one foot, as if the other one was too painful to depend on.

My eyes trailed down his body and stopped at his right hand, looking dark red with dried blood. I hadn't noticed at first, but the knuckles of his pitching hand looked misaligned, his fingers looking almost entirely incapable of moving. I closed my eyes and felt myself start to hyperventilate silently.

I can't do this without you, Silas.

Gerald took another foot closer, so close now that I could see him from my peripheral vision even when looking down at the ground. He was right there…

Please…

"Someone told me once that there's more to baseball than just winning," Silas said suddenly, his voice perfectly level. Gerald stopped approaching, seemingly taken aback.

"And what reason would that be?"

"The experience of playing on a team and helping your teammates as you learn and grow together," Silas scoffed at his own words. "That comes from a guy whose conviction and resolve was stronger than mine; he was able to get a solid hit on a fastball I wasn't holding back on."

Silas shifted his weight where he stood uncomfortably. I kept my eyes on the ground, afraid of what'd he'd say next.

"I ever tell you why I started to play baseball, dad?"

I tried to control my breathing as I gradually lifted my head up to look at Silas. He had turned his body halfway towards me, and he had his right arm fully extended. His index finger was pointed directly at the space between my eyes.

"It's because of *her*. She told me that a guy who can pitch a 100 mile-per-hour fastball was cool, and I wanted to be cool in her eyes. It's always been Clara."

Silas took a deep, confident breath. "My life would be pointless without her."

Silas turned to face his father again. "I won't turn my back on Clara, because there is no baseball to me without her," he declared, utterly devoid of any warmth.

"That's what this is about? Is it because I told you not to write to your middle-school crush? That's why you're disobeying me?"

"What?" I asked, my voice coming out no louder than a whisper. "You told him not to write me?"

"I should've never listened—"

"Silas! Come to your senses. You can still be with her if you want—no one is stopping you. I need that tape so that no one gets hurt, and I can keep everything I've built for you."

"You let them dump those criminals here," Silas spoke with an edge of ferocity. For the first time, Silas took an unsteady step towards his father, closing the distance between them. "She could have been hurt, and you didn't do anything to stop it. Her *mother* got sent to the hospital because of you. I'll never forgive you for that."

"I can see you've made your choice," Gerald said, disappointed. "Gerald?" Evelyn called out uneasily.

"That's fine. It seems like I'll have to address the person behind all of this directly instead," Gerald announced. He sidestepped Silas and stood right in front of me, causing me to take another frightened step backwards.

"How could you tell him to stop writing me...what

did I ever do to you—"

"Silas was distracted from his studies, his sports, just about everything. I needed him to focus on the here and now. I told him not to write to you so that he could move on. That is all."

Gerald rolled his shoulders backward intimidatingly. "I heard the police report on the drive over, Clara. I keep the local frequencies open." He paused. "Every single one of your little accomplices has been rounded up and is in custody. Some of them on the way to the hospital, like your friend in the woods."

I widened my eyes at him, a surge of panic in my heart. I knew what he was going to do; he was going to threaten me. The threat hadn't even left his lips yet and I already felt compelled to accept. Gerald's body alone scared me more than I'd ever been before.

"I can make sure to drag them all to Arden Bay's police station and keep them there, quoting an ongoing investigation. It'd be trivial, considering I had some local Fall River officers paid off. I'd drag out the investigation for as long as possible, keeping them away from their friends and families. You'd be prevented from ever seeing them as their case kept being postponed. Do you think I'm referring to months?"

I swallowed, hard. The fact that Gerald paid off local officers would explain how both kidnapping case and the advance copy containing that story were canned, as well as the police roadblock I ran into on the bus. I wasn't even safe in a different jurisdiction than Arden Bay.

Gerald scooped down to my eye level. Frightened, I walked back until I bumped into the desk behind me. Tears started forming in my eyes. I saw Silas stir behind Gerald, but Evelyn held him back by his arm. I could tell from his slack shoulders that there was no more fight left in him.

"Because I'm talking about *years*, Clara. They'll lose years of their lives, time they will never get back. All because they wanted to help you."

It looked like I wasn't as hard to read as I had thought.

Gerald had already figured out that I wouldn't care about being locked up myself and opted to threaten me with locking up my friends instead. Tears continued to fall down my cheeks as I ran through my options.

"What is it going to be, Clara? Will you abandon your friends, or will you give me the tape?"

"You'll let them all go?" I mumbled. I almost couldn't manage to get the words out.

"Clara, wait—" Audrey started to say.

"You have my word," Gerald answered.

"You can't trust him, Clara—" Silas tried to say, but Evelyn placed a gentle hand over his mouth, careful to leave his nose path open, to silence him.

There's no other choice.

My breathing continued shakily as I started to reach over on the table. I slipped my fingers under large sheet of paper that was covering a tape. I flinched as my fingers touched its surface, as if it burned me.

Everything I worked so hard for…

Gerald followed my hand and removed the page covering the cassette. He picked it up and tapped it against his head playfully.

I'm sorry, mom.

"This one, huh?" he asked. Gerald's eyes suddenly jerked to the left, to the desk space right in front of Audrey. He stood up and walked over to the desk and moved around the papers in front of her, revealing another tape.

"No!" Audrey howled as she tried to reach out to it before he swiped it himself.

"It's this one," Gerald announced. "But just in case…Dear, help me look through this office. I'm not leaving anything to chance. Grab any tapes you can find."

Evelyn and Gerald started to tear the office down, grabbing any cassette they found. They even searched all the garbage bins and under the desks. It was pointless hiding anything in the office itself; Gerald was thorough in combing the entire office. Audrey plopped down to her chair, looking devastated. She put a hand up to her forehead, her eyes glazed over and unfocused on anything.

I heard Silas make a strange noise, and I ran over to him as fast as I could.

"Silas—"

I almost didn't make it in time to catch him as he collapsed into my arms. I heard him give a hollow laugh.

"Sorry, Clara. Seems like my legs are giving out on me." He raised a shaky hand up to my back and held me against him. "Can't be more thankful for them, though. Since they brought me all the way back to you."

"Oh, Silas…"

"That's all of them, Gerald."

Gerald stood over Silas and me as he held up the cassette he had taken from Audrey. "Your help is appreciated," he said to me with an unfriendly look in his eye.

"Silas, I'm going to call you an ambulance. You're free to stay in this town for as long as you'd like, but when you're ready to get your life back on track, come back home."

Gerald started to walk away but stopped about halfway outside of the office. I bit back my tears as Gerald shot Silas a pitying look.

"You'll understand the sacrifices I'm making for you and their purpose one day. You'll come to your senses when you grow up," he said.

With that, Gerald turned resolutely to join Evelyn outside. Evelyn got into the car she arrived in—

"Silas!" Dana burst out of the car, running into the store and stepping on the broken glass. She got down and held Silas's mostly limp body next to me.

"She had me locked in the car, I couldn't come…" she trailed off. "Silas, I'm so sorry…I couldn't do anything…"

"It's over," Audrey said in a monotone voice. Her brow was furrowed, and she was leaning forward, her elbows on her knees, looking as if it was the stability given to her by her knees that prevented her from keeling over. All three of us looked in her direction. "He took the tape, our one and only piece of evidence. We're left with nothing."

"Clara, I might be mistaken…" Silas said with great difficulty. "But none of those tapes looked like the one I gave you—"

I winked at him flirtatiously as I pressed a hand against the less damaged side of Silas's face, holding it steadily. I planted a quick kiss on the side of his cheeks that was less hurt. Silas grabbed my hand and held it as he closed his eyes, as if my touch was the very thing that was keeping him alive.

"Not exactly," I said, getting to my feet after a beat. I walked over to Audrey, needing a moment to execute a small, necessary task. I slipped my foot out of my shoe, pulling hard on the inner lace until it gave. I reached beneath the arch and carefully pulled up the thin insole. There, perfectly concealed, was a tightly wrapped microcassette tape. I slid the tape from underneath the arch, quickly covering the insole back up, and relaced the shoe. Now that the small, hard lump beneath my foot was gone, I was able to stand comfortably again. I then took out the empty cassette player I had stored in my bag; the same one Silas had given me for my birthday.

I clicked the play button on the recorder, and the entire office grew quiet as Evelyn's recorded voice started playing.

"Oh—oh my god," is all Audrey managed.

"It's all thanks to you, Dana," I said as I looked over at her. She looked at me, a hopeful expression hidden past her tear-filled eyes.

"I heard your voice outside of the door. It's the only reason why I had enough time to hide the tape in my insole. You *did* do something, Dana. This would've failed if it weren't for you."

Dana hung her head. She wasn't saying it, but I knew that she was overjoyed. Tears sporadically fell to the ground by her knees as her shoulders quietly shuddered.

"Let's get to work," I said, shooting Audrey a confident look. I felt more determined than ever, and it seemed that my determination was infectious, because Audrey returned the look. She nodded at me in agreement.

***

Since we knew that Gerald and Evelyn would play the cassettes as soon as they got their hands on a recorder, we abandoned the office. We dropped Silas off at Fall River Hospital's emergency room along with Emmy and started getting to work in a different location.

Audrey and I worked as quickly as we could to gather all the evidence and prepare the feature. Since Audrey had her own column, she was able to dedicate the entire issue to the story. Additionally, due to her connections, we were successful in having the story published the very next day.

There were numerous legal consequences. In the weeks that followed, Fall River sued the city of Arden

Bay for damages, negligence, increased crime rates, and burden on their local services. The Mayor and everyone else involved faced immediate public outcry and outrage. Several forced resignations, impeachments, and recalls followed. Many lost all future political prospects, including the Mayor. Arden Bay also lost all additional funding it secured from the state and federal governments to penalize the city further. The city was deemed to be actively endangering a neighboring community for its own statistical gain, which greatly damaged its reputation.

Evelyn Reed received numerous criminal charges. She was charged with conspiracy, obstruction of justice, and numerous other charges. It was clear that she was being made the scapegoat and was receiving the hardest sentencing of anyone involved. This was understandable, since it *was* her voice that was heard in the recording, after all.

Gerald Quinn was brought in for questioning, but he wasn't incarcerated. It seemed as if Gerald disappeared from the limelight and managed to avoid the hammer of the law. Nor Silas or I heard anything more from him. It was very likely that he was waiting for the heat over the entire incident to blow over before daring to show his face again.

A few of the boys from the Fall River baseball team, who offered to serve as distractions, ended up in the hospital with minor injuries. Whether it be from pit maneuvers from the police or accidents when fleeing, none of these injuries were severe nor were any innocent people hurt. Everyone made sure to avoid any highly populated areas—not that any area of Fall River ever got too populated in the first place—to avoid any casualties.

Mason, who was also on the run, made sure to give up the chase before the things got too dangerous. He had Lauren in the car and didn't want her to get hurt, so they were uninjured.

Of the entire group, Silas and Caleb suffered the most injuries of all. Silas had numerous blunt force trauma injuries throughout his entire body. He had facial cuts and bruising, a swollen jaw, body aches and bruises in his torso, ribs and back, and had strained and sore muscles, especially in his shoulders and neck. Among all of his injuries, the most alarming to me were those in his hands. They were swollen and his knuckles were scraped and badly bruised. Even after weeks, his right hand was still painful to the touch.

Caleb's injuries were due to the violent crash of his Mustang when we were pit maneuvered. The lacerations and scrapes he had were nothing compared to the injuries he suffered to his head and his organs. The bleeding I saw from the side of his head was what I feared; a concussion from when he hit the window in impact. He had neck and back injuries and suffered from internal bleeding due to injuries to his organs, but thankfully it wasn't severe. The fact that Caleb was able to fight against the dizziness, nausea, and confusion caused by his concussion as he carried me in his arms was a miracle on its own.

Silas's recovery involved managing his pain, resting, and attending physical therapy for his swollen and bruised hand. The misaligned knuckles on his pitching hand were grave, and for a time it was starting to look like he would never pitch again. It was only after two grueling months of strenuous therapy that Silas was starting to recover significant amounts of his strength in his fingers again.

"It would've been worth it, even if I were never able to pitch again, you know," Silas whispered to me while he was still in the hospital.

"Don't say that…this is your entire career we're talking about," I breathed back.

"I already told you…There wouldn't have been a point to any of it if you weren't there to watch me."

Caleb required intensive care and an even longer extensive physical rehabilitation. It took him four months, and strenuous effort, to be discharged from the hospital.

Even still, I couldn't be happier that they both made a relatively full recovery, something that I started to believe wouldn't be the case for either of them. The *relative* in that statement is due to Silas's insistence that his pitching would never be the same. Try as he might, he was never truly able to pitch with the same speed he was able to exert before everything happened. Caleb suffered from strong headaches and dizziness from time to time, though thankfully these have lessened in frequency as the months went by.

All of the Fall River students that were arrested and aided in my escape were all absolved of any crimes once my story went public. The police department knew that the public outcry would increase, tenfold, if those who worked tirelessly to bring the truth to light were punished more than they had been already. There wasn't even anything added to their records, which was a tremendous victory.

Fall River initiated a large-scale effort to collect the released criminals from Arden Bay's prisons. A few prisoners who demonstrated an outstanding desire to fit back into society, like Mason's coworker at Cliff Point, were allowed to continue in society but were put under watch. Any slip up, and they'd be sent back to Arden Bay for processing. Most notoriously of all, the kidnapper that had kidnapped the young girl was tracked down and booked. This time, the law made sure he wouldn't be allowed to strike again.

More than a month had passed since Caleb was discharged, and yet my mother still broke into tears randomly.

"I—I can't believe you went through that all alone…" she'd cry as she'd be doing regular everyday tasks like folding clothes or cutting tomatoes.

I always took care to hug her when she got like that to comfort her when she needed it. "I wasn't alone, mom," I'd tell her soothingly. "I had Silas, and I had all of my friends."

"Besides, you were the one that went through something even more frightful than I did, mom. I'm just happy you're home again, and that I was able to get the truth out."

"Oh…sweetheart…" she'd say as her tears fell silently.

The paper was a tremendous success, and Audrey

sat down with me in her small office one fateful day. She already had the front door repaired, so it was no longer breezy throughout the entire business.

"I've never met anyone like you," she stated seriously. "Journalists could work lifetimes and not have what it takes to pull off what you've done."

I opened my mouth to humbly deflect my efforts and pass off some of the recognition to everyone who made it possible, but she wasn't having any of it.

"You're out of your mind if you think I'm letting you out of my sight. I can only imagine the places you'll go, Clara, and quite frankly, I want to be a part of it to see where exactly that is."

She extended her hand as if asking for a handshake. "Partner up with me. Let's run this column, *together*."

Just… help me be enough. No matter what it takes.

These were the words I would tell myself whenever I tried to believe that I could be community reporter. I heard the words as if a recorder was playing it back to me. I heard the faint click, as a recorder does when it's reached the end of its tape.

I reached out and gripped Audrey's hand tightly. "I look forward to learning from you," I told her. She was a much more experienced reporter, and I knew there were countless things she could bestow onto me.

Audrey gave me a content look. "Likewise," she answered.

More than six months had passed since Silas and my visit to Arden Bay. Silas and I walked side-by-side, alone, for what felt like the first time since the police chase. Counting hospital stays, concerned and fretting mothers, visits from friends, follow-up investigations from countless investigators, it seemed like something was always getting in the way between Silas and me getting some alone time.

Despite us having somewhere to be, I couldn't be happier that he was walking beside me, his hand comfortably fitted in mine. The warmth of it alone felt like it could keep me going forever, walking until the world simply ended and we both fell off it.

"Clara, listen," Silas spoke first, breaking the silence. "I want to apologize to you for everything my family has put you through. We both know they aren't going to apologize to you themselves, so let me do it for them. It felt like something was tearing me up from inside, knowing that my family was involved in what happened to your mother, Clara

"You could say they've been trying to hurt me ever since your father took you away from here, considering I felt abandoned by you" I said calmly.

Silas gripped my hand tightly, so hard that it started to hurt. Yet I didn't want him to let up at all. "That won't happen again. Even if we had to be apart, I'm not letting you go the same way. We'll write, call…no matter what."

I laughed despite the seriousness of the situation. "Yeah, I'd prefer that over you ignoring me in the weeks leading up to you leaving," I joked.

"Yeah, unless, you know, I just got tired and decided to stop writing you…" Silas teased. I bumped my shoulder with his playfully to shut him up.

I gripped his hand tighter, gathering the courage to say what I'd been meaning to tell him all along.

"Was what you told you father about me…true? That I'm the reason you started playing baseball?"

"I still remember it like it was yesterday," Silas answered. "You walked up to me on the first day of middle school and said that a guy that can pitch fast is cool. So, here I am."

"In fact," Silas paused, smiling teasingly at me. "You could say I fell for you right then and there. My feelings from that moment only grew, Clara. I was in love with you ever since."

"Wait…That day in the farmer's market, when you said, 'Nothing's changed,' what you meant was—"

"I was confirming for myself that my feelings for you hadn't changed."

I remembered the photo of me that Silas had in his bag, and the words he had written on the back of it.

The girl I've loved since the very first time I laid my eyes on her.

I smiled internally. Clearly, he wasn't shy about having admitted it at all. I wanted to one-up him by being bold myself.

"Silas, I want to tell you that I feel the same way about you, too. But it's not just that…there's more."

I tugged Silas's hand, pulling him to a stop. He stood right in front of me, giving me his undivided attention. Right at that moment, it felt like the entire world around us melted away and nothing else mattered except the two of us.

"Silas, I've been in love with you since back then, too. I've thought about you endlessly when you were gone. I—I put these walls up to stop myself from hurting…that's why I was with Caleb. But when you came back, it was inevitable that I started to have feelings for you again."

Silas opened his mouth, but I cut him off.

"You said something before, about baseball being pointless without me," I stammered, making Silas gave me a look of pure amusement. "Silas, I feel like I've been waiting for you to come back so that my life could truly begin. I think life *itself* would be pointless without you in it."

Silas pushed my hair gently behind my ear, giving me plenty of time to continue. I looked up at him defiantly, refusing to let my eyes leave his.

"Why didn't you ever tell me that your father told you not to write me?"

"He did tell me that, but what I told you wasn't a lie. I truly was afraid you'd write me back telling me that you had a boyfriend, and that your life was going well without me in it. So, I convinced myself it'd be best to now know about your life at all."

Silas massaged his neck. "Although, I couldn't help but find out some things. Like how I had found out you got that job in journalism. I couldn't have been happier for you."

I resolutely turned my head away from him with a *hmph* sound. "Regardless of us feeling the same way about each other, you still have to *formally* ask me to be your girlfriend, you know," I scolded. "So, hurry it up—"

Silas cut me off with a slow and passionate kiss. He pulled away after long, drawn-out pause, giving me a sincere look. "I won't waste any time, but I'm going to do it in the way deserving of you," he whispered quietly. I felt incapable of saying anything else, so I just nodded at him slowly.

"Hey! Lovebirds!"

I turned, blushing, to see Ralph calling out to us, waving his arms excitedly. We started walking closer, hand-in-hand.

"I'm really happy you agreed to do this," I told him, still flustered over the kiss. "I think it was about time that I tried it as a team sport and not something I was just being forced to do or something that I had to do just to win," he answered. "Besides, you're here watching me."

The Fall River baseball field was in view; the bleachers packed with students from Fall River and from the visiting team's school. Our friends were standing between the field and us, waiting for us to join them.

I caught Lauren and Mason holding hands as we approached. Lauren winked at me when I gave her a knowing look.

Knowing there wasn't anyone I could count on more for the job than Lauren, I immediately offered Lauren a full-time position as a photographer. Audrey was thrilled and didn't have any issues with the arrangement herself. Lauren readily agreed, meaning we'd be working together for the foreseeable future.

Emmy waved at us, which Silas and I returned. It was thanks to her gamble when we arrived at Audrey's office that Silas was able to find me. As she predicted, Silas arrived at the local paper unsure of where to go next. I'd been immensely thankful to her, since I would have had to deal with Evelyn without him. I had also caught her constantly eyeing Ralph more than a handful of times since the entire incident and had noticed numerous attempts to spend time with him alone. It was obvious that Ralph still hadn't gotten a clue yet, but it was only a matter of time before he realized she was interested in him.

I remember telling him just days before, "Thank you, Ralph, for everything," and meaning it from the bottom of my heart. Silas was with me at the time.

"Anything for my town and my friends," Ralph answered. Ralph's mother walked up to us from beside Ralph and extended her hand at Silas.

"Thank you, Silas, for your help that day at the store," Ralphs mother said calmly. "Thank you for meeting with me so that I can thank you properly."

Silas smiled as he extended his hand and shook hers. "It's no problem at all. I'm glad you're ok, and that I was there to help you when it happened."

This wasn't the only gratitude Silas received in person. I was able to convince Silas to meet with the kind old woman from the farmer's market, whom Silas assisted in getting back her stolen money.

"It was important for me to hear that," Silas told me, satisfied, after speaking to the old woman and to Ralph's mother. "I didn't think that I deserved appreciation or recognition. I just thought I was doing the right thing. But hearing them really opened my eyes that kindness really is appreciated."

I gave Silas a curious look when he said that. "I, uh…Growing up with my father, it was hard to hear someone thank me for something. I got used to people doing things not to be kind, but in order to get something in return."

Silas gave me a melancholic smile. "Trust me, I prefer believing in kindness, instead."

"So happy you're here!" Ralph said, giddily patting Silas on the shoulder. Silas smiled in response. I never thought I could be more attracted to Silas, yet seeing him for the first time in the Fall River baseball uniform almost made my jaw drop.

Caleb emerged from behind the group, his eyes lingering on my interlocked fingers with Silas. He smiled as he approached us. He raised his hand and offered a Fall River baseball cap.

"We'll be counting on you, pitcher," he said sincerely. Silas accepted the cap. He took off the cap he was wearing, which is the one with the bird logo from his middle school team, and placed the Fall River cap on his head in its place. Caleb and Silas then exchanged a brief look of mutual respect.

"Play to win and help those around you, not just to win—right?"

Caleb closed his eyes, amused. "Now I can say that we're on the same side."

Dana walked up to Caleb from behind and started tugging on his shirt playfully. "We should start heading there," she suggested as she gave Caleb a toying look. I noticed Caleb started to get a little flustered as he tugged on his shirt collar discreetly.

"Sure, let's go," he said, turning towards the field.

After Evelyn Reed—or, rather, Eleanor Quinn—was arrested, Dana had nowhere to live. She was old enough to make her own decision about where to move to, and she chose Fall River. She moved in with Silas and Lisette and was making the most of her time here.

It was shortly after she moved in that Dana told me that she had developed a crush on Caleb, one that only recently Caleb seemed to reciprocate.

I gave Silas a playful glance, curious about what his reaction was going to be once he found out about *that* development.

I waited behind as everyone walked towards the field. Ralph, Caleb, and Silas all had large numbers on their backs. I stared at the large number 24 on Silas's back and sighed, thinking about everything that had occurred ever since Silas came back into my life.

I looked off to the side, distracted, and noticed a familiar figure. It was the young man in fully black clothing and black curls. He was leaning on a light post comfortably. I recognized the man, and gave him an elated grin, somehow knowing that he'd be proud of me. The man smiled amiably back at me, a content look in his eyes.

Silas realized that I was lagging behind before anyone else and stopped walking. He waited and adjusted the cap on his head before gesturing me towards him. I smiled so hard that my cheeks started to hurt, jogging to meld my hand into his.

The three boys managed to secure Fall River a sweeping win, and as everyone in the bleachers riled themselves elatedly, I felt a hand reach over and squeeze my arm. It was Dana's, who was sitting just beside me. I looked over at her and saw a euphoric look in her eyes.

I looked over to the field where her eyes were looking at. On the field, at the pitcher's mound, Caleb and Ralph were hugging Silas and patting him on the back excitedly. I felt my heartbeat quicken as I remembered the words Dana once told me.

When I made that connection; that Silas got no enjoyment from it, I stopped watching his games. I couldn't take that look of his after every victory; a look that seemed that every victory was in fact a defeat in his heart.

And yet Silas bore a wide grin on his face, looking as happy as he did when I watched him play four years ago. That time seemed to dissolve into nothing when I looked at him. I took a deep breath as Silas saw through the entire crowd and made eye contact with me on the stands.

So? You think I'm cool, yet? His eyes seemed to ask. It was a question I knew he'd been meaning to ask all of these years, after all of his victories.

I've heard that love can strike twice, but nothing prepared me for the magnitude of this simple, blinding epiphany…

The miles I had walked, the danger I had faced to save Fall River, were nothing compared to the solitary, agonizing few inches I had to cross to reach the plain truth of my own beating heart:

The truth that I had fallen in love with Silas Quinn twice.

AFTERWORD

The question of whether this novel would have an Afterword was answered even before I began to write the story. Whenever I reached the end of a novel and I was met with an *Afterword* or an *Author's Note*, I always saw it as a bonus from the author to me, the reader, for finishing the author's work.

And so, you've come to find my bonus to you, dear reader.

When Love Finds You Twice is my debut novel; however, it is not the first story I'd ever written. Before publishing this story, I had already completed four full-length novels, all of which were shelved and hidden away, never to see the light of day. This means that anyone who may in the future decide to look up, "What was Thomas Bezombe's first novel?" will be met with nothing but disappointment.

I have used every bit of experience and knowledge gained from writing these four stories to create the work that is *When Love Finds You Twice*.

This novel has seen countless drafts. One major revision saw this story take on a completely new form. What was originally a story revolving around baseball and the antics of Clara, Silas, and Caleb evolved into a story of conspiracy, crime, and forgotten love.

If it weren't for the support I had from those around me, I would have never seen the potential this story contained and may have discarded it to join my other shelved stories. I could not be more grateful to them.

The more astute of you readers may have realized that the bird symbol used earlier in this book has no good reason for existing, considering there are no birds within this novel (apart from the bird logo on Silas' baseball cap). I assure you that there is a valid reason for the bird's presence! However, I cannot share the reason with you just yet. For now, please consider the bird to be the embodiment of the love between Clara and Silas growing wings and taking flight.

I have already said this multiple times, but I would like to once again reiterate my appreciation and deep gratitude for those who have beta-read this story. I can sincerely say this novel wouldn't exist if it weren't for them.

Lastly, I would like to thank you, reader, for picking up this story and for experiencing it. It is for you that I pick up my pen (or rather, type on my keyboard.) So, I thank you from the bottom of my heart.

ABOUT THE AUTHOR

Born in Argentina, **THOMAS BEZOMBE** is a bilingual Argentine American. He earned a B.S. degree in Information Systems Technology and currently works in cybersecurity as a red teamer while he pursues a M.S. in Cybersecurity. He lives in Florida, where he resides with his wife.